BROTHERS OF COLOR

A NOVEL

Tap Fore

Order this book online at www.trafford.com
or email orders@trafford.com

Most Trafford titles are also available at major online book retailers.

A special thanks to those family members who traveled with me on my research to The Lambertine
Plantation, The Mansfield's Battle Grounds and the city of Jefferson, Texas.

A special thank to Betty Morris and Spencer Meadow for editing.

Printed in Victoria, BC, Canada.

ISBN: 978-1-4269-2274-9 (sc)

*Our mission is to efficiently provide the world's finest, most comprehensive book publishing
service, enabling every author to experience success. To find out how to publish your book, your
way, and have it available worldwide, visit us online at www.trafford.com*

Trafford rev. 1/14/2010

 www.trafford.com

North America & international
toll-free: 1 888 232 4444 (USA & Canada)
phone: 250 383 6864 ♦ fax: 812 355 4082

Authors Note

This is work of fiction. Names, characters, places, and incidents are the product of the author's imagination and are used fictitiously. Any resemblance to actual persons, living or dead, business establishments, events, or locals are entirely coincidental.

A special thanks to those family members who traveled with me on my research to The Lambertine Plantation, The Mansfield's Battle Grounds and the city of Jefferson, Texas.

A special thank to Betty Morris and Spencer Meadow for editing.

CHAPTER 1

The Lambertine

In the late 1840's John Thomas Lewis had become a very wealthy man. He was a graduate of Baltimore School of Business and owned a large cotton brokerage business in New Orleans, Louisiana. He bought local cotton and made shipments to Europe. However, John found that the price of cotton was much less inland than along the coast due to transportation to port. Eager to capitalize on this advantage, he established a brokerage business in Camden Arkansas, as well as venturing into the slave trade. In 1850 he and his family, wife Ann, son Thomas, age eight and daughter Mary age eight months moved to Camden. Much of John's time was spent traveling the country buying cotton and arranging shipment to New Orleans.

On a buying trip from Camden to Fulton, Arkansas his travel took him through Columbia County. It was here that Lewis encountered a climate and soil that is ideal for growing cotton. However, with no rivers running in or out of the county, the only means of transportation was by wagon. The small farms of the local area bailed cotton at local gins and transported it by wagons to Camden and later shipped it down the Ouachita River when the water level would permit. Sometimes barges would dock along the river for weeks at a time, waiting for the river to swell and permit its journey to continue to New Orleans. The other option was to wagon the cotton to Fulton for shipment on the Red River to Shreveport and then continue its travel to New Orleans.

John realized a great business opportunity by establishing a large cotton plantation in the area. A railroad from the Mississippi River to the Red River at Fulton would provide a great opportunity for the local area to flourish with the cash crop of cotton.

In 1851 he purchased fifteen hundred acres of land located in southwest Arkansas and named the plantation "The Lambertine," after his favorite French poet. He hired an overseer by the name of Alfred Marlar and provided him with thirty one slaves for the development of the plantation. Temporary housing was built for his family. A number of slaves were busy building living quarters for them while others had begun to clear the land.

John moved his family into the temporary dwelling while construction of the main home began. Unfortunately, amidst the busy change, Mary became sick with the fever and died at age fourteen months old.

The home called "The Lambertine," was a large two story brick building. The brick were made and fire kilned at a nearby creek that provided the beautiful red clay. The interior of which was flanked with double stair cases leading to the second floor. An architect from London designed and decorated the structure, using mahogany on portions of the interior and in the construction of the furnishings. The finest carvings not ordinarily seen on the frontier adorned the interior. Thirty yards behind the main house, the kitchen and house-servants living quarters were built.

A group of ten cabins housing the thirty one slaves were situated about three hundred yards north of the main house. East of the slave camp stood two large barns that housed the wagons and farm equipment and the cattle feed. Northeast of the barns lay a pasture of approximately two hundred acres that held the farm animals, including the eleven mules, six horses, twenty sheep, twenty six head of cattle and seventy five hogs. South of the Lambertine were eighty acres under cultivation for vegetables and cattle feed. The cotton field consisted of approximately one thousand acres.

In 1854, John was heavily involved in the pursuit of bringing a railroad to southern Arkansas. His first railroad attempt through Columbia County was the venture of the Mississippi, Ouachita and Red River Railroad company. The company was formed and Mr. Lewis held stock as president. The line was to run from Gaines Landing on the Mississippi River to Fulton, Arkansas on the Red River. The route would link Camden and the Lambertine as well many other places along the way. Much of John's time was spent traveling to locate investors in the enterprise. He frequently stayed in living quarters at Camden, Arkansas and New Orleans, Louisiana near his cotton-brokerage businesses.

In the summer of 1857, John hosted a large barbeque at his home. The invitation list consisted of local dignitaries, the wealthy and most influential people of the area. A speech, calculated to arouse interest in the enterprise, was given. In it, John expressed his hope of being remembered as a railroad-builder rather than a planter, and in honor of the great enterprise, John presented his audience with four slave children, each being only a few weeks old. He named the children Mississippi, Ouachita, Red River and Railroad.

The stock company was subsequently formed by many citizens of the county and by many dwelling along the proposed route of the railroad. Cash and land were used as collateral to finance the line's construction. A right-a-way was secured and a considerable amount of grading was completed. Portions of the track were laid, including ties and steel rails, a short distance west of Camden on the eastern end of the line, but very little of the railroad was ever built. The railroad failed as a business venture about 1858 due to the pending war and the financial panic of 1857.

CHAPTER 2

Ben's Birth And Ann's Death

September 1858 was a very busy time for the plantation. The slaves worked from dawn until dark picking cotton. Two wagons continually made the three-mile-trip to the gin. Roosevelt and Dora, the house servants, cared for the Lambertine and prepared food for the Lewis family. Four slave women were responsible for picking vegetables, cooking and caring for the slaves and their children.

On September 19, Ann summoned Dora to quickly come to her aid. She had begun labor with the birth of her fourth child. Her labor however, evoked fear and concern. Already, one child had been lost at birth and a second, Mary, at fourteen months.

"Go to the field -n- git Phroney," Dora yelled to Roosevelt. "Mrs. Ann is havin' the young'un. Hurry!"

Roosevelt began to run toward the cotton field. In the distance he could see a swarm of pickers and a wagon about half a mile away. Alfred, the overseer, in the midst of circling and yelling at the slaves atop his horse, spotted Roosevelt running toward them and instantly knew something was wrong. He rode to meet him.

"Boss Alfred, git Phroney. Mrs. Ann is havin' that young'un."

With the message delivered, Roosevelt turned and ran back to the house. Alfred returned to the slaves and called to Phroney.

"Get up behind me, Mrs. Ann is in labor," Alfred commanded Phroney.

"No sir Boss, I ain't ever rode a hoss before."

"Put her black ass on this horse behind me," he ordered Achilles and Rubin.

"Boss, I scared, I might fall off."

"If you do, I'll stop and throw your black ass back up here."

He flanked the horse and traveled to the house in a gallop. Phroney, her arms tightly wrapped around Alfred's waist, cried from fright. They reached the house alongside Roosevelt, who helped Alfred remove Phroney from the horse. Accustomed to being a mid-wife for the slaves, she ran into the house and began shouting orders, helping Dora prepare for the birth. Ann's labor pains were about five minutes apart.

"She ain't ready yet, maybe several hours fore she has this young'un," Phroney informed them.

Roosevelt and Dora returned to their duties, anxiously waiting while Phroney cared for Ann.

At dark, the slaves returned to camp and put the animals away under the barrage of Alfred's orders. A few came to the house to help take food to camp, while others were feeding and caring for the livestock.

Ann's labor pains became more extreme by nine o'clock in the evening and Phroney had become very concerned. She summoned Alfred.

"Boss, she ourt to done had this child. Slave mammies don't have so much trouble. I think Th baby done turned -n- wrapped the cord around it. Sumpin' ain't right."

"Have someone harness the best horse and hook him to the carriage," Alfred instructed Roosevelt. "Have Big George go to Magnolia and bring Dr. Browning back as quickly as possible. Make sure to tell him not to run the horse to death."

Dr. Browning and Big George returned to Lambertine about six o'clock in the morning. The doctor was met at the door by Phroney.

"Doc. Sumpin' ain't right. I done hoped a lot mammies have young'uns -n- I ain't see's one have this much trouble without dying."

"Don't worry Phroney; Women have been giving birth this way since time began.

"Doc., she scared. She done lost one child when it was born and then another when it was a baby."

At eleven o'clock in the a.m., September 20, 1858, Benjamin Thomas Lewis was born. Later that day, John returned home and was thrilled to learn he had another son. He was however, shocked at Ann's condition. Dr. Browning informed him: "Ann's condition is very serious; she has lost a lot of blood. There is not a lot I can do but pray the bleeding stops, but I won't leave today. I'll stay and keep an eye on her."

After cleaning little Ben, Phroney told Roosevelt to go get Casalee to come and feed the baby. Casalee had a son of her own: Railroad, age one, still nursing, as well as Sam, three years old. Roosevelt moved to the slave quarters to care for Sam and Casalee moved into the servant quarters to care for Ben and Railroad.

Dr. Browning returned to Magnolia that afternoon. He told John he would be back early the next morning. He had left instructions with Dora on how to care for Ann. Dora did not leave her bedside that night. The next morning Dr. Browning returned and examined her. Her condition had worsened. He informed John of her extremely critical condition. Unfortunately, Ann died at 2; 00 p.m., September 22, 1858.

"I'm sorry John; I did everything I could for her. Is there anything I can do for you?"

"Yes, when you get to Magnolia, please go by the Funeral Home and ask them to come get her as soon as possible."

Shortly after dark, the hearse arrived. John and the undertaker meet for a short while and he selected a casket from a sales book. John asked Dora to get Ann's favorite dress and under garments for burial clothes. She was then loaded into the hearse along with her clothes and it drove away.

The hearse arrived near three o'clock the next afternoon. The slaves had prepared the grave site and she was taken for immediate burial. Some of the local people and the slaves had gathered for a short service. Ann was laid to rest by the side of her beloved Mary.

CHAPTER 3

The Civil War Begins

December 6, 1860, South Carolina was the first state to secede from the union. The federals were ordered to blockade the Charleston Harbor immediately to limit the Cotton Export to Europe. Three months later six other Gulf Coast States had also seceded. The federals were then ordered to blockade all Gulf Coast ports: the Mississippi River at New Orleans and the Colorado River at Galveston.

On April 12, 1861 at four o'clock in the a.m., General P. G. T. Beauregard gave the order to fire upon the federals that were holding Fort Sumter in Charleston Harbor. Within hours Beauregard and his seventy-five thousand Confederate volunteers were hoisting a Confederate Flag over Fort Sumter. This was the first shot of the civil war. Two days later four more states joined the Confederacy. The following order was issued by The Commander and Chief of The Confederate States of America: "All citizens between the ages of eighteen and forty-five are hereby ordered to report immediately for military duty at the court house of your respective county seat. Nonconforming citizens will be arrested and charged with treason." The order was signed by Jefferson Davis, "President of The Confederate States of America."

During this time, John was desperately trying to broker his large amount of cotton. It was in storage at Camden, Shreveport, New Orleans and other ports along the way. The cotton sales were very important to the Confederacy to support their war efforts.

He returned to The Lambertine in July to find that Tom had reported for military duty. Upset upon the realization of this news, John summoned Alfred and the two met on the north field.

"Why in the Hell did you let Tom enlist, Alfred?"

"I tried to talk him out of it. I told him he had to stay and help me and look after little Ben. His only reply was: "You and Casalee can take care of him. I need to go help General Dockery whip some Yankee asses."

"God damn you, Alfred," John yelled. "I feel like beating the hell out you."

"Why, hell John! What was I supposed to do? He is eighteen and just as stubborn as you."

"You should have had the slaves hog-tie him and lock him in the corn crib or something until I came home. You should never have let him go."

"John, you might as well calm down. He would never forgive either one of us if I had done that."

In a very soft voice John conceded to Alfred: "I know you're right." With that, he turned and walked to the carriage with his head bowed. The carriage turned and carried him toward the house. In the distance Dora walked down the hill caring little Ben with Roosevelt following shortly behind.

"'Look -a- here child," Dora softly spoke to Ben. "Look who has come to see ye." John stepped from the carriage and took Ben into his arms. With a growing smile on his face, he hugged him close. "Ben, it looks as if it's only you and me that are left for a while," John whispered as a small tear fell from his chin.

Walking up the stairs into the house, John and Ben were accompanied by Railroad who ran along their side. "Railroad, ye come here," Dora yelled to him. "Ye know ye ain't supposed to go in the big house." Railroad looked to her with a gloomy look on his face.

"It's alright Dora. He will be fine."

"I ain't ever let him go inside the house before, Mr. Lewis. Ain't no black supposed to go inside cept me and Roosevelt."

"Who told you that?"

"Mrs. Ann, Sir."

"It's alright, Dora. Mrs. Ann ain't here anymore," John replied.

"Master John, let me take him to the back door. Ain't no black supposed to go through the front door." Looking down at Ben, John replied: "He is part of the family, ain't that right Ben."

Dora went to the kitchen for a tray of refreshments and returned to the company of John, Ben and Railroad who sat in the comfort of the sitting room.

"Only one glass? What about my little friends." John looked at Railroad and asked if he was thirsty. Railroad nodded his head yes.

"Master John, don't ye spoil my boys," Dora quietly complained as she went to fetch two more glasses from the cupboard. She returned to the room and filled a small glass for little Ben. Dora was addressed by John.

"Dora, prepare the center bedroom for Ben and Railroad. They will be staying there when I am at home."

"Master John, it ain't proper fur a nigger to live in the big house."

"I'm the one to say what is proper and what is not."

"Lord a mercy, you going to have them white folks takin' cause you let a nigger live with you."

"Dora, I don't give a shit what they say," John retorted. "Bring their toys to the center bedroom." After a while Ben became fretful and began to yawn.

"Master John, It's time for Ben's nap."

Within seconds, Casalee came through the door of the sitting room. Ben, crawling as fast as he could, went to meet her. "Com'on Ben, time to eat and have a nap. Tell ye Papa bye" Casalee said as she waved at John. Ben waved as he was scooped up by the arms of Casalee and the three left the room.

John sat in silence as a saddening feeling overcame him. He was reflecting on the sure disappointment Ann would hold against him. He had allowed Tom to join the military, but most troubling Ben's well being was cared for by the black slaves. As tears began to run down his cheeks, he began to pray and shortly drifted off to sleep.

Near dark, he was woken by a light tapping on the door. He yelled, "Come in Dora." She opened the door.

"Boss Alfred is about done with his work, ya'll ready for supper?"

"Sure, have Roosevelt bring a bucket of fresh water to the serving room."

"He done did that."

"Has Ben and Railroad already eaten?"

"Yes sir, a long time ago."

"We'll bring your supper," she said as she walked away.

John went into the serving room and was washing his face and hands as Alford entered.

"John, how are you feeling?"

"Better, it's been a long day," he replied. "What's for supper, Dora?"

"Ye favorite. Corn bread, pinto beans, mash taters and ham. If ye save room, I done made some fried apple pies."

"Thanks Dora, it's nice to be back home."

After they had eaten, John loaded his pipe while Al rolled a Prince Albert. They sat quietly for a few minutes before Alfred broke the silence. "How ye doin' John?"

"I don't really know," John murmured. "I feel that God has forsaken me. I'm not a praying man, but I feel that everything is going wrong. I prayed for Ann and James when he was being born, and James died. I prayed for Mary when she got the fever, and she died. When I came home after Ben was born, I prayed for Ann and Ben, and Ann was lost. I prayed today, but I did not mention Tom. I just can't lose him too. All I ask is that he gives me guidance as to what to do with Ben."

"I'll see ye in the morning," Alfred remarked as he rose to leave. "Oh John, I almost forgot. Mrs. Martin came calling last week. She wants to talk with you about an important matter. I knew it wouldn't be long before the widow women would start calling," Alfred added with a chuckle.

"Hell, Al she's almost old enough to be my mother. What did she want?"

"It's you, John," Alfred replied as they both laughed. "She had written you a love note, I'll go get it."

Returning to John, Alfred handed him the note. It read:

Dear Mr. Lewis,

I would like to meet with you as soon as possible concerning a matter that I feel is of great importance. Please let me know when you return home.

Yours truly,

Mrs. Effie Martin

John read the note and turned to Alfred. "What the hell is this matter of great importance?"

"May be love making on her mind."

"Get the hell outa' here, you got work to do. You meet me here at seven in the morning," John barked to Alfred as he went out the door laughing.

The next morning at breakfast, John handed Alfred a note, the surface of which detailed the way in which Big George was to take the carriage and deliver the enclosed message to Mrs. Martin and wait for a reply. "She lives in the big white house in the curve, on the left, before you get to Delta. If he don't know where, have him come see me. The enclosed message to Mrs. Martin read:

Dear Mrs. Martin,

I am sorry that I missed your calling, but I would like to meet with you at any time of your convenience, maybe for dinner tomorrow. If that is not a good time, please reply with a time that we could meet. I will arrange to have a carriage pick you up whenever you are available.

Sincerely,

John Lewis

Big George retrieved Mrs. Martin as planned and they arrived at the Lambertine about ten thirty in the morning. Mrs. Martin was met by John at the carriage and escorted into the house.

"Very lovely home, Mr. Lewis."

"Thank you, but call me John."

"You may call me Effie if you wish, John, you know how the people talk about the neighborhood. We are aware of the demands your businesses make of you and the time you must appropriate to them. I have come to offer my assistance for Ben. If you must leave, I would be happy for him to stay with me while you are away. We all know he is being raised by slaves and are assured that they are taking good care of him. He needs, however, to be living with white people. He will learn to talk with the gula accent and you don't want that."

"Thank you, Mrs. Martin. This has been a terrible time for me. This war has put a stop to the development of the railroad, which I plan to complete later. Now is a very crucial time for my cotton business. There are a lot of problems exporting because of the blockades and I must devote some time to salvage the business. I have given orders to my people. If the Federals overtake Shreveport and Camden they are to burn all my cotton in order to prevent the Yankees from obtaining it. As for now, I plan to stay close to home as much as possible and take care of Ben. If however, I must leave suddenly, Dora and Roosevelt are very capable of taking care of him."

"I'm sure they are but John, he needs to be with white folks or he will speak as the niggers do when he gets a little older. John, I don't want to step out of line, but you must consider letting me take care of him and provide some schooling.

"Effie, neither of us are spring chicks anymore, and you don't need the burden."

"I didn't want to bring this up at this time John, but my daughter Elsie would love to take care of him. She and William have been married eight years and they want a child, but I guess it is not God's will. She has said she would move here to take care of him if you would permit."

"Where does Elsie live?"

"Jefferson Texas, her husband is a Baptist preacher there."

"Mrs. Martin, you don't know how much I appreciate your concern. I have thought many times of my options and they were few. Now I know that maybe there is a solution. Now, I think Dora has dinner waiting. Are you hungry?" "Starved" she said as they went into the dining room. Nothing more was mentioned about Ben during dinner.

Later in the evening John confided to Effie. "Mrs. Martin, I feel very much alone without Ann, and Thomas is with Dockery's Nineteenth at God knows where. I can't give Ben up just now. I do appreciate your offer to help and I will call if the occasion arises. I would like to thank you very much for coming, and please feel free to call any time."

"Thank you very much Mr. Lewis, I mean John," she said as she walked out the door.

That evening when Alfred came to supper the Conversation turned to Mrs. Martin. "How was your date?"

"It wasn't a date. She was concerned about Ben and offered her help."

"You told me that you prayed for help with Ben, maybe your prayer is being answered."

"Maybe it is."

CHAPTER 4

Thomas Killed Oct 4, 1862

About two in the afternoon on October 21, 1962, John was setting at his desk when Roosevelt came to the door. "Master John, there is two riders coming up the driveway."

"Are they in uniform?"

"Yes they is."

"Thank you Roosevelt. I have been afraid of this day. Would you take Ben and Railroad to the slave quarters," he said as he went to the door. He was standing on the lower step as the riders approached the hitching rail.

"Are you John Lewis, father of Corporal Thomas P. Lewis?"

"Yes, I am. I'm afraid that you are bearers of bad news. Am I correct?"

"We are very sorry, sir. Yes, we are. I am Champlain Specialist Jim Roberts and this is my assistant Tom Waters. We are here at the personal request of General Thomas Pleasant Dockery, 19ᵗʰ Arkansas Infantry."

"You men get down and stretch your legs," John requested. He then yelled for Roosevelt to care for their horses. "Would you like to come inside?"

"That would be nice; we have been in the saddle for several hours."

They entered the house and took a seat. Chaplin Roberts removed a letter from his coat pocket and handed it to John. "General Dockery told us he was from the vicinity of Lambertine and regrets that he never had the opportunity to meet you personally. He added that he would make a special effort to meet you after the war. I know that he was very fond of your son and as busy as he was, he wanted to take time to write you. If you will excuse us, we will visit your outhouse and give you a few minutes alone."

"Yes, thank you." John sat for several minutes before opening the letter, thinking to himself. "If I had never gone to New Orleans and stayed home where I should have been, this would have never happened. Al should have never let him join, damn his soul" After a few minutes he remembered what Alfred had said about there being no way to stop him. He then opened the letter.

> *Mr. John Lewis,*
>
> *I am writing this correspondence with a very heavy heart. I knew Corporal Thomas Lewis, your son, personally. We had conversation many times of the people of Columbia County, as that is my home. He was an outstanding solider and conducted himself gallantly. The Arkansas 19th was in route to support General Fredrick Steele at Pine Bluff when we encountered Federal Troops at Mark's Mill. We were victorious, although we suffered an estimate of two hundred*

and ninety casualties and the Federals suffered approximately nine hundred casualties along with four hundred prisoners. The battle ended at mid afternoon October 4. It was of utmost importance that our army continues our advance to support General Steele. Specialist Jim Roberts and sixty troops were assigned to remain behind and clear the battle field. To my sincere regrets, due to time restraint, the casualties are buried in a mass grave, with the exception your beloved son Thomas. His body was taken to a Baptist Church in Marks' Mill for interment. The grave is located in the south/east corner of the cemetery and is marked. You will be contacted at a later date for other arrangements, if you so desire for his remains to be transported to some other place for burial.

Thomas was under the command of Lieutenant-Colonel W. H. Dismukes at the time of battle. I asked Dismukes to report any availably details of the battle. His report is enclosed.

I have the honor to be, very respectfully, your obedient servant.

General Thomas P. Dockery

******

Report to:

General T. P.Dockery

Ref. Corporeal Thomas Lewis.

"I desire to call to your attention the pre-eminently gallant conduct of Corporeal Thomas Lewis, who during the entire engagement, kept twenty to thirty yards in advance of his regiment, using his gun with good effect. He was mortally wounded by a rifle shot to the chest. Unfortunanly, he became a casualty within a matter of minutes."

Colonel W. H. Dismikes –

A few minutes, Specialist Roberts returned carrying a canvas bag with a wire seal. "Luckily, we were able to recover Tom's pistol and a few personal effects such as his wallet and a few other items. Mr. Lewis, if you don't mind, would you sign this receipt for me that you received this bag and the seal has not been removed" Jim said as he handed him a receipt book.

"I'll be happy too, but this seems a little unusual" he said as he signed the receipt.

"You'll be surprised of the amount of thief that takes place among the troops. This is for my protection. Therefore they will know I did my job. If you will excuse me, I will join Tom out back" Jim said as he walked away.

After a few moments of reflection, John went into the back yard and began visiting with the officers. Ben and Railroad saw them and came running to John.

"Is this your son?" Tom asked.

"Yes, he is all I have left. My wife passed when he was born. We lost one at birth and another at fourteen months to the fever. It's hard for a man my age to raise a three year old child. I guess it wasn't meant for me have a large family.

The two children stared at the officers, and Railroad asked, "Is

Mr. Thomas dead?" Roberts looked at John and he slightly nodded. "Yes." Roberts replied "Yes, Mr. Thomas was killed in battle. He was a very brave soldier."

John and the officers watched for their reactions. Neither of the children said anything for a while, and then Ben said, "I want to be a soldier someday." After a few seconds, Ben ran and got his ball from under the Chinaberry tree and threw it to Railroad. A short time later, all were engaged in catching and throwing the ball around. There was no more talk about Thomas.

"Ben soon will be living with another family. He needs an education that I am afraid I cannot provide. Dora, Roosevelt and Casalee, Railroad's mother, takes real good care of them, but neither of them can read or write. I don't know what I'm going to do with Railroad" he said jokingly. "They are like brothers." Changing the subject, John asked of the soldiers: "Are you boys from around here?"

"I'm from Sutton, Arkansas and Tom is from Minden, La."

"How did you receive this duty?"

"Well, Mr. Lewis, I'll tell you the truth. I ain't afraid of getting killed. What scares me is killing someone else. Tom and I will do anything in our power to help the south win this war except fire upon another, even a Yankee. Maybe it's our religious belief. We have spied, ran through the battles delivering messages with bullets flying all around, but we just will not carry a gun. I just can't do it. They keep us away from the front-line battles because they know we would not survive the first advance. We would never be able to pull the trigger. They classified us as 'specialist,' conscientious objectors. Most troops call us cowards. We will do anything they ask of us except fight. We spend a lot of time cleaning the battle field, helping the wounded and cleaning up after the surgeons, which is the worst job. This is one of the easiest duties. This is like being on a vacation."

"Do you have several notifications in this area?"

"Yes sir, we have others in this area, and then we will hurry to catch up with our division. Sir, you may know some of the families, but I'm not at liberty to tell who they are."

"I can understand. I had rather hear from you than through the grapevine."

"I'm very sorry Mr. Lewis, If you like I will pray with you or anything I can possible do to help."

"That won't be necessary, but there is one think. Do you ever personally see General Dockery?"

"Only a time or two, but if you have a message for him, I'll get it to him."

"If you ever see him, give him special thanks from me. Will you?"

"I sure will."

"You boys have time for supper with us, and possibly stay the night?"

"Yes, thank you. We would love to if it is not imposing. We have hardtack and bacon in our saddle bags, but you can imagine what it is like."

"I would be hurt if you didn't join us," John said as he yelled to Dora to prepare for two guests.

"We have another notification a short distance away, but we couldn't get there before sundown. We are not allowed to notify after sundown, therefore, we would be camped in the woods waiting for daylight. Sometimes I spend several hours with the love ones while Tom finds a relative or neighbor to stay with them. We will not leave them until they can control their grieving."

"You don't know how much a personal notification means."

Roosevelt came to them and announced that supper would be served shortly. "Are the kids eating with you tonight?'

"Yes, have Dora set them a place."

John saw Al at the barn and went to tell him of the news. After a few minutes they returned to the house. He introduced Al to Jim and Tom. During dinner that night the conversation was very light. No one mentioned Thomas's name.

After dinner John and Specialist Roberts went into the sitting room. As John was filling his pipe with tobacco, Tom said "I'm a tobacco chewer myself. If you'll excuse me, I would like to sit on the front porch for a while."

"Oh, please make yourself at home," John said.

"I'll join Tom," Al said as he and Tom went out the front door.

Tom explained the details of Tom's death and his burial. "We had two hundred and ninety causalities. One hundred and eighty killed in the field. That sounds bad, but the report was that the Yankees had approximately nine hundred causalities. We took about four hundred prisoners. Clearing the battle field was quite a chore."

"Were you on that detail?"

"Yes, Jim and I both were. We had sixty of our troops and used about one hundred of the Yankee prisoners for clean up detail. This was a welcome assignment to get away from that duty. General Dockery ordered that Thomas's body be taken to the "Smith's House", which was being used as a hospital. Several local residents came to help, which is always appreciated. The women went to help the wounded and the men helped us with the burial. A local planter had brought twelve of his slaves to help dig the grave. We were glad to see them. We carry the bodies to the gravesite and the staff members search and record all data they were able to retrieve. Some can't be identified, therefore, if they miss roll call, they were listed as "Missing in Action". Our army is always short of footwear; therefore we removed the boots, if they were worth keeping, and collected what firearms we can find. Many times the bodies had been robbed before we could get to them and that makes identification almost impossible."

"How long did it take to clear the battle field?"

"This one took about, three days. They were scattered over one half mile by one mile area. There were a lot more Yankees than rebels. What makes you feel strange is that you are trying to kill a man one day and then the next day you are working next to him removing the dead. We would place the rebels in one area and the Yanks in another until the wagons could haul them to the burial site. The graves are on opposite sides of the battle field. We had a supply wagon in the battle field for the arms and boots. We had our dead buried before they had theirs and then we helped them finish their job. Sometimes we would have lunch together and swap jokes. One common thing is trading tobacco for beef jerky. Those Yankees know how to make good jerky," he laughed and added "one of the jokes was "this jerky is worth killing for."

"I'm sure by the third day, the bodies are unpleasant to handle. The odor must be terrible."

"It's not as bad as you might think or maybe it's something a person gets used too after a while."

"Shall we go inside and visit with John and Mr. Roberts? I know this has been a long day for you. You may be almost ready for bed."

"We left Camden before day light and had a notification at McNeil which didn't take long, but to answer your question, I'm about ready for a good soft bed."

When they entered the door, John said "What was that I heard about a good soft bed?" The beds are waiting whenever you are ready. If you boys would like, I could have Roosevelt fill the tub with warm water, if you'll like a bath."

Tom looked at Jim and asked with a big grin, "How long has it been since you had a warm bath?"

.   "Hell, I can't remember when I had the last bath, but I do remember it was in the Ouachita River and it sure as hell wasn't warm."

John rang the bell and Roosevelt appeared shortly. "Take the tub upstairs to the north bedroom. Draw water and have Dora heat some for these boys's bath. If you would like Dora could wash your clothes and hang them by the stove to dry."

Jim said, "No, No, absolutely not. We carry an extra changing of clothes and were able to get the other set washed at Camden last night. Thanks very much, but we are in good shape."

Roosevelt was busy carrying water up the stairs. He stopped and said "First bath is ready, sir. Towels are on the chair."

Tom said "I don't mind volunteering to be first. Is that O. K. with you Jim?

"Sure, we don't want to fight over it and destroy this man's house. Git up there and wash your nasty ass." They were all laughing as Tom raced up the stairs.

A few minutes later Tom Yelled "Next" and Roosevelt immediately raced up the stairs with an empty bucket.

Jim said "Roosevelt where you going with that bucket?"

"Gonna change that water. I heard you say he had a nasty ass. You need clean water." He dipped the water from the tub and poured it out the window. He then began to refill the tub. On his last trip up the stairs he stopped, looked at Jim and said "Sir, your bath is ready."

As Jim was going up the stairs, John said "Breakfast will be ready at day break, but you can eat any time. You all have a good night. See ye in the morning."

The next morning after breakfast, Roosevelt brought their horses to the front hitching rail. They were saddling up when John came to the front porch and thanked them again for their kindness. "If you see General Dockery, thank him for me and tell him I'm looking forward to his visit."

As they were mounting to leave, Dora came with two bags "Ise done gone 'n' fixed you's boys sumpin to eat after while. I knows what ye got in that saddle bag ain't fitin to eat."

They took the bags and said "Thanks Dora," as they rode away.

Al asks John "Do you want me to go get his body and bring back here for burial?"

"No, let him rest where he lies. I will order a tomb stone; you can take it and put on his grave site. That's all we can do for him." John turned and walked away.

CHAPTER 5

Raid

By January of 1864, the plantation was in financial ruins. The Mississippi, Ouachita & Red River Railroad Company was bankrupt and the stock worthless. The vast amount of cotton owned by Lewis was in storage. No buyer would gamble to invest in any of John's business ventures due to the blockades and risk of the cotton never reaching the open seas for shipment to Europe.

The slaves were spread through the plantation doing winter chores, repairing and building new fences, cutting fire wood and clearing new ground for cultivation.

The first of February a cold front swept across the area, causing the temperature to drop to near freezing. After eating supper that night, John conversed with Alfred.

"Al, we may have some ice tonight. I don't know of a better time than daylight in the morning to start killing hogs."

"I agree, how many you think we should kill?"

"Less plan on three or four tomorrow, but if the cold weather holds, maybe twelve or fifteen in all."

By the First of March they had slandered sixteen head. The hams, shoulders, middling and bacon were covered with salt and seasoning and hung in the smoke house along with the sausages.

John and Alfred were having supper when there was a light tapping on the door. "Come in Roosevelt," John said, his ear accustomed to the sound of his tapping.

"Master John, there is a rider coming down Military Road, I think he is coming here."

"Thank you, Roosevelt," John said as he walked to the window. He went out to meet the guess.

"Get down and come in," he called as he motioned for Roosevelt to care for the horse.

"My name is Robert Crank. I live over near Dourcheat Bottom."

"Please come in and I will have Dora fix you a plate, would you be our guess for supper"

"I would be more than happy to be."

John introduced him to Alfred and asks of his guest: "What brings you over this way."

"Well, I don't guess you have heard, but there is a large group of Yankee soldiers crossing Dourcheat Bottom. Some have already started marching up Military Road this way."

"Where are they going?"

"I don't know. They came through Old Washington about ten days ago. A man has preceded them, warning those in the Yankee's path of their arrival. He had said that he had asked where they were going and the leader told him: "It wasn't a damn bit of his business and to keep out of the way and keep his damn mouth shut."

"How many troops are there?'

"Can't say for sure but the man told me near two thousand, mostly black and they have about fifty wagons. They are having hell getting them through that waist-deep mud.

They are spread out about six miles. Rumors are they are going to Camden or Shreveport."

"I'm sure our troops know they are coming,"

"There have been dispatchers sent to both places. After a good night's sleep, I will head toward Camden and inform the people what is taking place."

"Well, thank you for informing us. I'll show you to the guess room where you may make yourself at home. I will call you about daylight when Dora has breakfast ready."

When John returned he motioned for Alfred to meet him outside.

"What ye think, Al?"

"I really don't know. If they are on the military road, they will come by here."

"To be on the safe side, don't say anything until after he is gone tomorrow. I think he is on the up -n- up, but he may be scouting for them. Have you ever heard of him?"

"The name is new to me, but after he leaves I will ride that way and find out if he is for real."

After breakfast Mr. Crank continued his travel going east on military road. Alfred rode west toward Dourcheat Bottom. After traveling about three miles, he meets a carriage with a white man and a Negro driving the team.

"Have you seen any Yankees troops?"

"Yes, there are several hundred this side of the bottom and more coming across."

"Where are they going?"

"I don't know. Robert Crank told me he thought they were headed to Camden or Shreveport."

"Do you know Mr. Crank?"

"Sure, I have known him for several years. He has a small spread north of Falcon toward Brockman Hill. He is on his way to Camden to warn people they are coming. By the way who are you?'

"I'm Alfred Marlar, overseer of The Lambertine."

"Sure, Mr. Marlar, I have heard a lot about you but, never had the pleasure of meeting you in person. My name is Orville Wicker; I live just this side of the bottom about one mile south of military road."

"Well, thank you for the information and stop by the Lambertine for a visit."

"I'll be happy to do that."

Al turned his horse around and road back toward Lambertine with the horse at a gallop. In a short while Mr. Wicker was out of sight, trailing some distance behind.

When Alfred returned he met with John. "Mr. Crank is on the up -n-up. He lives between Falcon and Brockman Hill. I met Orville Wicker, he had seen the troops and they are headed this way."

"Have Rubin and Big George catch eight mules and the best two horses and take them into the woods behind Shiloh Church and tie them good, if they get loose they may come back home. Cut the fence and drive half of the cattle and the hogs into the woods."

"Why, only half and not all of them?"

"If we leave some of the cattle it will not look suspicious. Have Achilles load half the meat from the smoke house into a wagon and take behind the Flaritie's Place into the woods. Tell him to take blankets with him because it will be cold tonight. He is to stay until someone comes and gets him. Have the women take brush brooms and erase the tracks. Tell the slaves to stay in the cabin area, away from the troops. If they are asked anything, tell them you know of nothing more."

"Maybe they will march on by," Alfred suggested.

"Don't count on it."

The next day, by mid-morning, the army was seen marching from the west on the military road headed toward the Lambertine. The army halted as four riders came riding up the hill toward the house. John and Alfred went to meet them.

"I'm Cornel Williams, commander of the Kansas Infantry and the Indiana 14th battery division."

"I am John Lewis and this is Alfred Marlar. Would you'll like to get down?"

"We are scouting the country in search of forage for the federal troops at Camden," Cornel Williams said as they dismounted their horses. "The supplies are about exhausted. Our troops have been on half rations for about three weeks and the citizens of Camden are also running low. You will be given a voucher for what we take and will be paid a fair market price."

"Bull shit, we both know I will never receive a damn dine."

"Mr. Lewis, I'm only following orders, if you don't want a voucher, that is fine with me, but we will take what we need. We will leave you enough to survive."

"Take what you must have. All that I ask is that your troops stay away from my people and stay out of my house. We have a large supply of fire wood, tell them to help themselves and if we run out they can cut the trees. Please ask them not to burn the rails from my fencing."

Williams turned to an aid. "Notify the troops of Mr. Lewis

request and post sentries around the slave camp." He then looked at John. "Mr. Lewis, I will suggest to them not to burn your fences, but we are fighting a god damn war and if we damage anything it will be added to the voucher." The aid turned and went to the bivouac area. The troops were busy erecting tents and caring for the animals.

"My staff and I would like the use of your house tonight, with your permission, of course."

"You are welcome to use the first floor with my permission. Although I feel you were going to use it anyway, right?"

"We will never know because you agreed."

A wagon was driven and parked near the front porch. Aids unloaded several boxes of files and placed them on the dining table.

"Mr. Lewis, would you please excuse yourself," Cornel Williams requested.

"This is my home, what if I refuse?'

"I'll arrest you and have you detained. Things will be better if you grant my wish, don't you think so?'

John started from the room, and then said: "If you and your staff will be my guess for dinner, I'll ask Dora to prepare for you."

"Sure we would like that. Eating from the back of a wagon gets old after a while. A home cooked meal sounds good, that is if you and Mr. Marlar join us."

Jokingly, John asked, "Are you afraid we may poison you? How many are on your staff?"

"Five of us, the other one will arrive later."

As John went by the kitchen he told Dora and Roosevelt to prepare for five extra dinner guest. He then joined Alfred at the barn and watched as the troops loaded his wagons with the content from the corn crib.

Near dark, Roosevelt rang the dinner bell and John and Alfred went to the main house. John came to the dining room and announced that dinner would be served shortly. They began to re-pack the boxes and cleared the table. Roosevelt came and began to set the table. He took the drink orders: a choice of water, tea or milk. Williams and his staff then carried the boxes back to the wagon. They returned to the serving room, washed their hands and sat at the table. When John and Alfred joined, Williams introduced them and informed them that the other member would arrive shortly. The front door opened and the man from the carriage, the man who had previously told Alfred his name was Orville Wicker, came through the door.

Williams introduced him as Captian Robert Van Dyke. Alfred refused to shake his hand and said "You lying son of a bitch..."

"Sorry about the lie, but we are fighting a war and I will do whatever I must to be victorious. You asked me to stop by sometime. Bet you did not think it would be so soon."

"I suppose the man named Robert Crank, is also a spy."

"No, he is doing us a favor but don't realize it. I follow him and then watch where you hide your belongings."

John said to Williams, "You said you would leave us enough for us to survive. Your men have empted the corn crib and the smokehouse."

"We have recorded what we have taken including your two wagons and the mules. You still have the supplies that you hid in the woods. We will also take the livestock in the pin because you have released enough to serve you into the woods."

As they were almost through with dinner, there was screaming noise and gunfire coming from near the slave quarters. Williams, in a calm voice, told one of the aids to check out the rifle fire.

John and Alfred hurriedly got up and started toward the door. Williams told them to sit back down.

"You go to hell, I have a son down there and I am going to check on him."

"I said sat down."

"I said go to hell, I'm going down there. Shoot me in the back, if you don't like it, you worthless bastard," John yelled as he walked out the door.

John found that three black troops from the Kansas Infantry had attacked Cherry, a young slave woman. Jackson and Rubin were fighting the two soldiers off to release her. Jackson reached for an ax and hit one of the soldiers in the back causing serious injury. The guards opened fire on the group that were fighting, injuring one of the soldiers and killing Rubin. Cherry had escaped into one of the slave cabins. The soldiers had surrounded the action and broke up the fight. The three soldiers involved were taken in to custody. The aid reported the action to Williams.

"How badly are they hurt?

"One has been gut shot and another is unconscious with a large injury to the back. I'm sure he had broken ribs and lung damage. An ax was buried in his back. The other involved is not injured. One of the slaves was also killed."

"Take them into the woods, kill and bury all three of them. Get information on all three and make out a report accordingly. You may note that they were killed crossing a sentry line. I don't see that the execution is worthy of mentioning."

When Casalee heard Cherry scream, she ran with little Ben and Railroad to the graveyard and hid in the trees. There, they huddled together until they heard John calling. All three cried from fright. John took Ben and Railroad to the big house. As he walked past the federal officers, John remarked: "Your boys made a hell of a mess of things tonight; I'm putting these boys to bed."

The slaves had built a large fire to provide light and brought a table from the barn. They wrapped Rubin in blankets and laid him on the table. A circle was formed around the table and songs of mourning continued throughout the night. The next morning the body was taken to the slave graveyard and buried. As they returned from the burial they could see the troops marching east on military road.

Ben and Railroad became permanent residents of the center upstairs bedroom next to John's room.

CHAPTER 6

Red River Expedition
April, 1864

Jefferson, located in Marion County Texas, known as "The River Port to the Southwest" is situated on Big Cypress Bayou, approximately 46 miles from Shreveport. Steamboat traffic was possible because of a log jam on the Red River.

The river flowed around the jam creating swamps and lakes, forming parallel waterways and raising the water level of Caddo Lake and Big Cypress Bayou sufficiently enough to allow for navigation into Jefferson. The ships would travel from New Orleans by the Red River into Big Cypress creek, across Caddo Lake, then into Big Cypress Bayou. Steamboat traffic into Jefferson averaged over two hundred arrivals per year, with an average carrying capacity of four hundred and twenty-five tons each. Freighters would sometimes set in the basin for two or three days before getting to the dock for unloading and re-loading. The exports were primarily cotton, maize, processed beef, hides, leather products, shoes and iron products.

Marion County had a population of approximately twelve thousand, one half being slaves. There were two hundred thirteen slaveholders in the county and Jefferson was home to the largest slave livery in Texas. Many were auction and shipped to west Texas and New Mexico. Slave owners were concerned of a Confederate defeat; therefore, they were disposing of them before they became freed.

April 6 1864, the Union Army left Natchitoches on the last leg of its journey to capture Shreveport and destroy the city of Jefferson Texas.

Major General Nathaniel Banks was hopeful, even confident, that the sixty-mile trip would take only four days. His army would capture Shreveport and continue to Jefferson and destroy the city and block the shipping path with fallen timbers. His army had met little opposition from the Confederates. He knew his troops out numbered the Confederate two and one half to one. He was convinced the Confederates wouldn't stand and fight.

He chose to take the inland road toward Shreveport, although a road did not exist along the Red River that would have allowed support from Admiral Porter's Navel Fleet. The rules of a traveling army were to keep the baggage wagons at the rear. For sake of convenience, Banks placed the baggage wagons behind General Lindley Lee's Cavalry and in front of three infantry divisions. Another supple train was placed before the last two infantries of Maj. A. J. Smith's Guerilla. The first cavalrymen set out at the head of the column on Thursday morning and Smith's Guerilla, didn't fall into place until Friday, with the cavalry already twenty miles down the road.

A few miles from Grand Encore, the army marched out of agriculture country and into a dense pine forest. The road narrowed to little more than path in some places. It began to rain. It fell hard all day and the soldiers trudged ankle deep in mud. The Confederate Cavalry, under the command of Brig. General Thomas Green, had taken place in the woods and began to fire on the singles in the strung-out line of Lee's cavalry, which was defenseless. They were ordered to dismount and pursue the attacking force. The confederates vanished into the dense forest. The march continued and the sniper fire returned again causing Union casualties. Lee request that the three hundred wagons be sent to the rear in order for the center infantrymen to advance position. General Banks denied the request. The center infantries were to protect the rear of one supply train and the front of the other.

During the night, April 8, Col. Frank Emerson's First Brigade advanced to the front to help support Lee's cavalry. They continued the march with the confederates contesting every step.

Confederate Lt. Gen. Richard Taylor requested of his superior, Gen. E. Kirby Smith, to advance to Sabine Crossroads, three miles out of Mansfield. The Moss Plantation was set in a clearing 1,200 yards wide and 800 yards deep with a large hill in its center. Smith gave him permission to set up defense but not to attack until he was given orders. Taylor took position and when the union center infantries reached the crossroads, he knew this was not only his best chance to defeat Bank's army; it was also about his last chance.

They waited. Taylor had 8,800 men, but he was expecting another 4,400 Arkansas and Missouri troops marching as reinforcements from Keatchie, twenty miles away. By mid-afternoon the troops had not arrived and Banks' army had not taken offensive positions. With the day growing late, Taylor didn't wait for orders from General Kirby

Smith, he ordered an advance. He knew that the Federals weren't about to start the fray. Taylor knew Lee's cavalry and Emerson's Brigade were eleven miles north and would have to march in the mud past two hundred wagons on the narrow muddy path. General A. J. Smith's Guerillas were south by eight miles and wouldn't arrive before darkness.

After dark, both armies were in desperate need of water. Taylor and his men had gathered at Emory's creek, a short distance away. That night the Yankees marched twenty miles to Pleasant Hill to a water supply. The rebels spent a good part of the night counting their winnings; twenty artillery pieces, ammunition and small arms, one hundred loaded wagons, and one thousand horses and mules. The Confederates lost 1,000 men killed and wounded; the Federal lost more than 2,200.

During the night the 4,400 Arkansas and Missouri troops arrived. Taylor and his troops marched to Pleasant Hill in pursuit of Banks' army. The union troops had set up a strong defense and the armies were at a stand off until the middle of the afternoon. Taylor ordered an attack and the battle lasted until darkness. The rebels had given way one regiment at a time against the point blank volleys and clubbed muskets. They ran with the Yankees chasing and whooping after them for three miles. The Confederate army was defeated on day two of battle with 1,600 dead and wounded. The Federal had 1,300 dead and wounded.

The next morning the armies retreated in opposite directions. Although Banks recovered from the disaster at Mansfield with a satisfying victory at Pleasant Hill, in the end the Confederates won. Shreveport and Jefferson were safe for the present time.

CHAPTER 7

Ben And Railroad Began School

June 1864, John and Al discussed schooling options for Ben and Railroad. They would work with the boys in the evening after the daily choirs were complete, but by then it was almost bed time for the boys. John realized that he and Al would not be able to provide proper schooling. There was a lady at McNeil, nine miles away, who was teaching a few elementary age children in her home. The nine mile trip in the morning and again in the afternoon would be very tiring for the boys, but that was the nearest schooling available. John contacted her about enrolling Ben and Railroad. She would gladly accept Ben, but not Railroad. She told John that black kids were too slow to learn and they would interfere with the advancement of the other children. John disagreed and knew he had to find another way. Al suggested that he contact Mrs. Effie Martin and ask for her help.

John paid Mrs. Martin a visit. She saw him as he was coming to the door. "John, it's nice to see you. Want you come in?"

After the greetings, John got to the reason for the visit. "Mrs. Martin, what brings me this way is that once you offered to help me with Ben. He is 5 and Railroad is 6 years old. Al and I have been trying to teach them to read and write. I don't think we are doing a very good job. I was wondering if you may be able help?"

"John, there is nothing I'd rather do. I'd love to teach him. I'll come to your place or you can bring him here."

"Effie, maybe you misunderstood. I said him and Railroad."

She had a surprised look on her face and said, "Railroad, also. I don't know a black in the country that knows how to read and write. I'll be happy to also teach him."

"It's hard for a black to get an education in the south. If we lose the war, which looks like we may, they will become free and shortly there will be schools for them. I want Railroad to know how to read and write also. They are always competing with each other and I think they will do better schooling together. If you can please help, I'll pay you two dollars a week or more if you like."

"Oh, John, that will be more than enough. We'll need supplies."

"I have some supplies, although we may need more later. I have enough to get started. They know some of their ABC's and a few of the numbers. As I said Al and I have been working with them but at night when we find time they are tired and ready for bed."

"I have been worrying myself thinking about that child, wondering what you were going to do."

"I can't give him up now, but I have been thinking about your daughter, Elsie. Do you think she may consider boarding him later?" After the battle at Mansfield, I think the threat on Jefferson has ceased.

"I know she would. That would make her and W. S. the happiest couple in the world. They want a child, but that isn't in God's plan."

"What is a convent time for you? If you need more time to think about it, I'll make the time whenever you like. I was thinking maybe three afternoons a week, two or three hours a day."

"No, No, that's not enough. Let it be Monday through Friday from nine in the morning until three o'clock in the afternoon. That will give me time to prepare their lunch each day. I may need to teach them some table manners," she said laughing. "I'm so excited. When can we start?

"Is tomorrow soon enough?"

"That will be great, I'll be waiting"

"I'll have Little George bring what supplies I have this afternoon and I'll bring them tomorrow and maybe spend a little time with them. They may be a little nervous the first day. I can remember my first day many years ago," he said with a smile.

John stood and started toward the door. He turned and put his arms around Effie and said, "Thanks, you have answered my prayer".

As he was leaving he said, "By the way, what is Elsie's last name?"

"It's Crank. Her husband's name is William but everyone calls him Dub."

"Is he related to Robert Crank?"

"That's his dad."

"I met him the day before the raid, a very fine man," he said as he walked away.

John told Al of the arrangements he had made and he could tell Al was very pleased by the big smile on his face. "I'll tell the boys after dinner."

John and Al were enjoying their 'after dinner smoke' when Ben and Railroad entered the sitting room with their tablet and pencil, expecting their schooling. John said, "Boys, there won't be any schooling tonight. You'll start a real school tomorrow. Mrs. Effie Martin will be teaching you. She is a better teacher than Al and I. You'll be in school from nine o'clock in the morning till three o'clock in the afternoon."

Ben had a pleasant expression on his face but Railroad had a sad look. After a moment of silence, Railroad said, "Master John, I don't want to go to school. I want you to teach me."

John was surprised to see Railroad's reaction. He could tell Railroad was very nervous about being taught by Mrs. Martin. He told him of her, where she lived and what arrangements had been made. Railroad repeated again,"I don't want to go school."

John said, "You need to go to keep Ben out of trouble. I don't want to force you. If you are going to live here in the big house with Ben, you will learn to read and write or you can take your cloths and move into the slave camp with Red River. Which do you want to do?"

With his head lowered, in a very soft voice he said, "I'll go to school."

John and the boys arrived at nine o'clock. Effie had the class room set up with a small table, two stools, an ABC and number posters attached to the wall. She also had a cardboard clock with movable hands on the wall. She handed John a piece of paper and said this is our schedule. "You don't have objections to my reading Bible stories on Monday and Wednesday afternoon, do you?"

"Of course not, thank you for including it. That's something Al and I haven't done. It looks like you have everything under control." He then whispered to her, "Railroad is very nervous,"

She began to quiz the boys on the letters and numbers. After a few minutes John said, "Looks like everything will be fine. I'll see you boys later," he winked at Effie as he went out the door.

John was there at three o'clock and they came running to the carriage. They yelled, "Bye Mrs. Effie". She had a big smile and waved bye as they drove away.

With a big smile Ben said, "Railroad almost got into trouble today."

John looked at Railroad who was also smiling, "What did you do?"

"I said to Ben, its bout time for yo papa to come git us." Mrs. Effie told me not to talk like that. She made me say five times "It's about time for your father to come get us." She told me to never say bout, yo, papa or git again or I would have to set in the corner." They all laughed about Railroad almost getting in trouble the first day.

John was happy to know that their grammar was going to make a vast improvement.

CHAPTER 8

John Plans Trip

By June 1865 the Lambertine Plantation was in severe financial condition. The banks were pressing foreclosure on the property. They would no longer accept the slaves as collateral, which had an appraised value of $14,700 when the loan was taken in 1862. At that time John's brokerage business had 6,680 bales of cotton in storage. The federals had confiscated 2,140 bales and John had ordered 1,255 bales destroyed and the balance of 3,285 bales were hidden in various locations along the Red River, Ouachita and the Mississippi Rivers. The railroad stock had become worthless.

After supper Ben and Railroad had went upstairs to their room and John and Al were enjoying their after meal smokes. "Al, I'm in very serious financial trouble. I just can't see any way to save the Lambertine. I have a few thousand bales of cotton hidden, but have no buyer or any way of selling them. My big concern is Ben."

"John, I hate to say it, but it doesn't look like the south is going to win this war. It's going to be hell for the south if we lose."

"I don't know what the slaves will do. I'm sure some will hang around and some will go back to Mississippi and Louisiana where they came from, but they will not be able to find work in the South and the North won't want them. They will head north by the millions."

"It will serve the North right if they are freed; they will then have to feed them. You know the slaves may starve to death by the thousands. It won't be good for them."

"If the South wins, I'll have to sell them to pay the bank, maybe I can save the home, but there is no way to save the property. For example, Achilles was worth $1700 in 1862, now I would be lucky to get $200 for him. I understand there are some buyers in Jefferson Texas who are shipping them to New Mexico. They could be hidden there for several years before being freed. They had better hurry because they may be free in a few months. I had rather free all of mine, rather than sell for that price."

"What are you thinking?"

"Now that Shreveport and Jefferson are no longer under threat, I have got to figure a way to sell what little cotton I have left or Ben will be left with nothing. I need to go to Jefferson and New Orleans to find a buyer and a way to get the cotton to the open sea. I might be able to ship by land to the Sabine River and then export from Port Arthur. The Federals may not have a blockade there. Europe is offering a good price once it has passed the blockade."

"Ben and Railroad are seven years old now. Mrs. Effie has done a wonderful job with them and she seems to really enjoy teaching them. Mrs. Effie's daughter has said many times she would love for Ben to live with her. It will break our hearts to send him to Jefferson to live, especially Railroad. Her husband is a Baptist preacher and I know they will take good care of him. I don't want him to move now but maybe when I return. He is safer here at the Lambertine than in

Jefferson, although I think the Federal threat is over for now. I can operate my business better from Jefferson than here. I will look for a home while I'm there. You can handle things here."

"I will soon be leaving for Shreveport, Jefferson and New Orleans. I expect the war to be over in a month or two, the south being the looser. If that is the case and the Federals lift the blockade, I may be able to ship several hundred bales of cotton quickly. I'm not sure how much there is in hiding or how much has been stolen or destroyed. My Men were to keep me informed and I haven't heard from them lately. I have a few hundred bales hidden below Camden, maybe they are still there. I will visit Effie tomorrow (Sunday afternoon) and tell her of my plans. See to it that Ben and Railroad attend her schooling while I'm gone."

"I will have Roosevelt and Achilles pack the carriage and I'll leave early Monday morning. I will take Little George with me as my carriage driver. He is about the same size as Thomas, so have Dora get some of Tom's cloths and alter to fit him. Tell him to shave and get a haircut. I don't want him looking like a slave. We will be gone for at least two months. There are a lot of robberies taking place on the road. I will carry some money but Little George will wear a money belt with most of the cash. Have Achilles put a small metal box under the rear seat of the carriage, in such a way as to hide it. I will put a few hundred dollars of Confederate Notes into it and maybe they will think that is all we have. If we are robbed, which I expect we will be, they will ask Little George where the money is hidden and he will tell it's them under the back seat. They would never think to search him. When they find it, maybe they will get excited and leave us alone. They may search me and take what little I have but Little George will be carrying the bulk of the money."

"If it happens, I hope Little George will not panic."

"He won't, I just hope we are not robbed twice. There are a lot of deserters out there from both sides."

Sunday afternoon John visited Effie. He told her of his plans and informed her that he would be away for almost two months. "They will attend school as usual. If there are any questions, contact Al and he will make any required decision."

"John, why not let them stay with me? They can stay in my extra bedroom and we could get in more schooling."

"Thank you for the offer, but that will be too much for you. My servant takes very good care of them and I don't want to disrupt their lives now. They are making such good progress. I would like for him to be a little older before I have to find boarding for him. I think to separate them would be too emotional for them. I hope Elsie is still willing to take him in another year or two."

"John, she will be thrilled for him to live with her. I will do anything I can to help while you're away. If Al or Dora need me for anything have them let me know."

"Thanks Effie, I don't know what I'd do without you."

"John, before you leave I must show you something. As a matter of fact, I was planing to contact you to show you something wonderful." She went and got a stack of papers. I asked the boys to draw a cat. Here are their drawings. Ben's cat didn't turn out so well, but not bad for someone his age. Look at Railroad's cat. I was amazed how good it was. I then asked them to draw the clock on the wall. Here is Ben's, average for a boy his age, but look at Railroad's. The circle is almost perfect; most engineers can't free hand better circles. The numbers are symmetrical about centerline and geometrical positioned perfectly. Look how clear the numbers are and the hands look just like the ones on the clock. Railroad has a God given artistic talent. We must do everything in our power to help him develop it. We don't want him working cotton for the rest of his life.

"This is amazing. I have attended a few drafting courses and I for one can appreciate his talent. I will order some elementary books on art or maybe I can find some while in New Orleans. He may have a great future in front of him, if we do our part. I'm so happy you discovered his God given talent. I will mail you the books as soon as I can find them. I must go and pack for my trip. Thank you for everything."

As John was walking away Effie said, "John, have a good trip and I will be praying for you because I am quite worried about this war."

CHAPTER 9

Highway Robbery

After arriving in Shreveport, John visited with Paul Cooper, his business manager, and office employees. The cotton count was near what he had expected. He ordered his men to locate as many barges as needed and prepare to ship the cotton down river. They were to ship at night and dock during the day in any tributary large enough to float the barges. "I will return in four or five days and check on the progress. Little George and 1 need to go to Jefferson for a while. "

One of his employees said "John, you'll need to be careful. There are a lot of rebel deserters that are robbing everyone they see on the highway."

"We have been warned and we'll just take our chances. Would you help George unload our bags, we will be traveling light." He called George aside and told him to leave the box under the back seat.

They were a few miles out of Jefferson when they meet three

Rebel Soldiers. One stopped the horses and the other road to the side of the carriage. "Are you Yankee spies?' one of them ask.

"No, I'm not a Yankee spy, please step aside and get out of my way."

"Boys, it looks like we have a tough one here." He leveled his rifle across his lap pointed at John. Mister you don't understand, we are assigned to check everyone traveling this road. Are you carrying any money? There is a charge for traveling this road and I think it best you pay up."

"I am not carrying any money; I have been told there are lots of you low life bastards robbing on the highway."

One of the others pointed his rifle at George and said "I hope your Master doesn't piss us off, that wouldn't be good. Boy, where is the money?'

"Mister, there ain't no money."

"Don't lie to me. It would be bad if this gun accidently went off. Where is the money? You'll need to pay the toll."

Little George said, "Look under the back seat."

One of the robbers dismounted and looked under the back seat. "Hey boys, look here. I guess the master forgot this was back here" as he opened the box."

"How much is in there?'

"A lot, looks like four or five hundred" as he flipped the notes.

John said, "Four hundred and eighty dollars to be exact. Take it and get the hell out of our way."

"Four hundred and eighty ain't enough. The toll is five hundred dollars; looks like you are a little short. I think if you drop that fancy pocket watch in this box and give us the money from your pockets that will be close enough."

John removed his watch and placed it into the box and handed him the few coins he was carrying. "Now get the hell out of my way."

They stepped aside; laughing one of them said, "Yawl have a good day. It was nice doing business with you. We are doing our job for the confederate army. You'll need to be careful; there are some robbers out here robbing people."

John flicked the reins and told the horses to "Get up." They drove away without looking back. He asked George, "Was you scared?"

"Yes master, I think I pissed in my britches."

John looked at him smiled and said, "I know for sure that I pissed in my pants. You did a good job George".

"Too bad they took ye watch."

"That watch wasn't any good. It's been broken for a number of years. They probably know that by now. Those Confederate Notes are worth 15 cents to the dollar. They think they have five hundred dollars but got less than a hundred"

When they arrived at Jefferson, there was a lot of activity at the slave livery. One slave was receiving a whipping. George had a startled look on his face. "What is going on master?'

"The slaves had run away from the plantation. They have been captured and are beind sold. They are shipping them to south Texas and New Mexico. All of you will be freed in a few months when the war is over. It will be several years before they are found and freed. You stay with me, don't get out of my sight. I don't want to lose you or the money you are carrying." There was three wagons leaving the livery with ten shackled slaves in each and was being followed by a supply wagon. The wagons were escorted by deserted rebel troops.

John parked the carriage in front of J. H. Benefield's Law Office. He went to the door and he told George to stand just inside the door where you can keep an eye on the carriage. If anything happens, call but don't you go outside. He then went and asked to see Mr. Benefield. His secretary said "I will get him, who shall I say is calling?"

"My name is John Lewis."

A few minutes later Benefield appeared and asked John to come into his office. After entering, J. H. started to close the door behind them.

"I had rather leave the door open, if you don't mind."

J. H. had a strange look on his face and said, "Not at all. What can I do for you?"

John explained his credentials and reason for being in Jefferson. "I need to open a few accounts in the bank here and I want you to administer them. I am a lawyer myself, but I need someone else to handle them. If you are interested, maybe we can pay the bank a visit.

"Sure, I'll be glad to help you, if I may ask, why this bank and not your bank in Shreveport?"

"I have checked out the bank and I understand you are a minority share holder and I am aware of its assets and officers. If Mr. Loerwald is in, maybe we could meet him this afternoon and take care of business.

"Let us walk over and see. We'll be at the bank for a while," he said to his secretary as they walked away."

As they walked by George, John said, "Follow us."

They went to the bank and asked to see Mr. Lowerwald. "He is not in today but the Bank Manager, Mr. Miller will be happy to assist you."

They were escorted into his office and introductions were made. J. H. looked at George and asked John, "Would you like for him wait outside?"

"No, he does not get out of my sight."

John explained his reasons for opening three separate accounts. One would be called "The W.S. & E Crank" for $500, another "The Baltimore Law School for $1200 and the last a saving account for Benjamin Thomas Lewis, a minor, to be administrated by J. H. Benefield for $4000. Do you gentleman think you can set them up?'

"Sure, we can take care of them. How will you fund these accounts?

"Gold" John replied.

"When will you be able to fund them?'

"Immediately, as a matter of fact, now if you would be so kind as to give me receipts, we will return later to sign the finial papers."

They looked at each other and J. H. said, "Surely you are not carrying that much gold with you."

"No I'm not, but George is; I'm sure he is ready to get rid of the weight. Is that right George?"

"Yes Boss, It done got heavy."

"Remove the belt and let us count the money." The money was counted for each account. George then replaced the belt with the remainder. John then asked "Does that feel better George?"

"It sure do." he replied.

Mr. Miller handed John the receipts and he and George went to the Jefferson Hotel for a room.

They walked to the registration desk and John inquired about a room. The clerk looked at George and said, "You are welcome, but he will not be able to stay here. We don't allow niggers. He will have to sleep at the wagon yard."

"May I see the owner of this hotel?"

"He is unavailable, I can get the manager. You can discuss it with him."

"No, I don't want to talk with the manager. I want to talk to Mr.

Loerwald. I understand he lives on the top floor and I would like for you to get a message to him that John Lewis is waiting to see him. You may mention that I'm president of The Mississippi, Ouachita, & Red River Railroad."

A few minutes later Mr. Loerwald appeared and offered his hand to John. "Mr. Lewis I have heard quite a lot about you. Aren't you not a cotton broker, owner of the Lambertine and I know quite a lot about the Railroad. As a matter of fact I own stock in the M.O. & R. R."

"Yes, I also know a lot about you."

"What may I do for you?"

"My body guard and I need a room and your clerk informed me that George will have to sleep at the wagon yard. I'm hoping you will make an exception to the rule."

"I can't do that Mr. Lewis. Once I let a nigger sleep on one of the beds and word gets out, white people will refuse to rent from me."

John reached into his pocket and removed the receipts and handed them to him. "Your, Mr. Miller and Mr. Benefield are doing the paperwork on these accounts as we speak. I was hoping we could take care of this matter this afternoon, my bank at Shreveport would be happy to accommodate me. It is a matter of convenience to use your bank and also your hotel. George will only need a blanket and pillow; he is use to sleeping on the floor. We must be in the same room for security reasons. If you would have your clerk get me a key and have a blanket taken to that room, I'll not take any more of your time."

He looked at the clerk and said, "Put them in an executive suite." He then looked at John and asked "How is the railroad business?" Him knowing that the business was in bankruptcy.

"You didn't have to ask. You know it is in bad shape right now, but in a few years it will be more profitable than your slave smuggling business." He then looked at the clerk and said, "Would you help George with our luggage. I'll be waiting outside."

Loerwald was red faced with anger at John's remark but just stood there chewing on his cigar without saying anything. John walked out the door.

John and George visited the Cranks that afternoon and then went to the bank to sign the banking agreements. Early the next morning they returned to Shreveport.

After arriving at Shreveport, John went shopping for school supplies, children books and books on drawing. He then went to his office to check the progress his staff had made on shipping the cotton.

Eight barges were already loaded and two other were waiting for cotton in route from up river. "When will the shipment be ready? John asks.

"We'll need two more days. We are still waiting for two more barges coming up river. They should arrive here about same time as the cotton coming downriver. That will total twelve barges, with 60 bales each, a total of 720 bales. Is that too large a shipment to risk?'

"No, I think one steamer can handle all twelve barges. If we split it we will have to locate another steamer. If things begin to look dangerous, we will split in route and have to go back and forth several times to make delivery. Would you get word to Butcher at the Camden office to ship everything they can locate boats and barges for?"

John said to one of his staff "I have been told a paddle wheeler is leaving in the morning for New Orleans. I will take it and plan on the cotton being there in thirty or forty days. Will you have one of the employees take George to the Lambertine and bring my horses and carriage back here?"

"Sure, consider that taken care of."

He gave George the schooling supplies and told him to see that Mrs. Effie received them.

CHAPTER 10

Ben Moves To Jefferson

John contacted Elsie and W.S Crank, Mrs. Martin's daughter and son-in-law, and asked if they would come for a visit. He explained his intentions and they were thrilled for Ben to live with them. They came to the Lambertine for a two week visit in order for Ben to become acquainted with them. Railroad was moved back to the slave quarters.

At the end of the visit, Ben's belongings were packed. John thought the parting would be less emotional if the slaves went about their regular duties. After the slaves were in the fields, Roosevelt and Dub loaded Ben's trunk and other belongings into the carriage. Ben sat between Dub and Elsie. Their farewells continued until the carriage moved out of sight. Although Railroad had been instructed to stay inside the cabin, he had escaped and ran behind the carriage until it neared the Military Road.

"Bye Railroad," Ben shouted. Elsie told him to turn around and look straight ahead. Dub tapped the horses with the reins to increase their gate. They never looked back, not knowing how far Railroad followed.

Within the carriage, nothing was said for several minutes. Finally, Ben broke the silence.

"Roosevelt told me and Railroad to be big boys and not to cry. I bet Railroad is crying."

"Ben, sometimes it is alright for big boys to cry," Elsie responded. "Do you think it would make you feel better?"

"Yes Mama," he replied.

"Well, I'll tell you what to do," Elsie said calmly as she put her arm around him. "You put your head on my lap and cry all you want to."

Ben lay down on the seat, put his head on her lap and began to cry very softly. She looked through teary eyes at Dub and saw his eyes had become teary. Ben began feeling a strong bonding with her. Casalee had held him close before, but never had he felt the affection as now.

Ben had never been away from the Lambertine except for the few times Roosevelt had taken him and Railroad fishing at Dorchete Creek. He was enjoying the scenery of the trip and became excited when they entered Magnolia. As they passed the cotton gin and commissary he looked with great interest.

"Is that my dad's cotton?"

"Your dad may own a little of it, but most is owned by a lot of different people."

"I have never seen a gin or so many wagons and mules. As a matter of fact, I have never seen so many people at one time."

Else looked at him and said: "You haven't seen anything yet. Wait 'till we get to Jefferson. You will see a lot more people, a lot of cotton and some ships. You are in for a surprise." He looked up at her with a big smile on his face.

They arrived at Jefferson three days later, late in the afternoon. As they passed the "Slave Livery", Ben saw three slaves with leg shackles and a chain locked to a hitching rail. He had never seen a slave shackled before. He had never thought of slaves being bought and sold. The Lewis slaves had been on the plantation all his life, and he did not think of them as a commodity.

"Why are they chained to the rail?"

"To keep them from running away. They probably ran from their last plantation. Their master has brought them here to be sold. The new owner will take them to another plantation." Elsie replied.

As they neared the pier, Ben saw a large freighter docked and many slaves were being un-loaded from one ramp and a heard of cattle from another ramp. There was a commotion coming from the pier with loud shouting. They looked in that direction and saw a slave was being lashed with a long whip. Elsie told him to look the other way. He turned the other way with a sad and puzzling look on his face. He asked no questions.

After a few weeks, Ben was excited to be at Jefferson. He had made several new friends and was enjoying the town activities and school. He was over whelmed by the new environment, although he thought of Railroad often.

After Ben's departure, John conducted his business as usual, traveling to New Orleans trying to dispose of some of his cotton. Two months later, he had found a buyer and had smuggled most of the Louisiana Cotton to Port Arthur in Texas. It was loaded aboard a freighter and reached the open sea.

He received payment and went to Jefferson to see Ben and take care of business with Attorney Benefield. While he was in Jefferson, news reached him that General Robert E. Lee had surrendered at Appomattox, ending the civil war. John purchased a home in Jefferson and immediately returned to Lambertine to close his affairs there.

CHAPTER 11

Ben Begans Loan Business

After the war, the blockade was lifted. John had already managed to smuggle and sell his cotton-in-holding to Delta Cotton, a European company. Cotton was in great demand due to the reductions of output during the war. He hired a fleet of cotton buyers and listed cotton purchases throughout Texas, Louisiana and Arkansas. By 1872 his holdings amounted to several thousand bales of cotton, some being held in warehouses, and a constant flow being shipped along the Mississippi, Ouachita, Sabine and Red Rivers. During this time he was also promoting the M. O. & R.R. Railroad. His short visits to Jefferson were sometime at six to nine month intervals.

Ben had his fourteenth birthday during John's absence. He received a birthday card and letter, postmarked in Jonesville, La. John was apologizing for his long absence and offered to Ben an increase of allowance to $25. That was an extremely large allowance for a fourteen year-old boy, but John wanted to make sure he had adequate spending money. Ben already had a surplus of cash and his friends were well aware of his financial superiority. He was to make small, short-term, interest-bearing loans. The increase in allowance allowed him to increase his loan business. He and some friends were at the pier, a favorite past time, when he was approached by a friend, Doyle Atkins, a dock worker, with a business proposition. Tourist and local people had inquired at the dock many times about row boat rentals. There weren't any row or fishing boats available for rental. Doyle asked for a $100 loan to purchase six boats.

"I think it is a good idea. I'll talk to Mr. Benefield about a contract but you know $100 will cost you $125 this time next year?"

That was Ben's first large loan. By age 16 he had in excess of $1000 in notes receivable.

CHAPTER 12

John Dies

John returned to Jefferson to spend Christmas and New Year holidays with Ben. He decided to try to liquidate his cotton business and devote his time to development of the railroad. On February 20, 1873, he departed for New Orleans to negotiate with a European Cotton Company, d.b.a. as "Delta Cotton Company." He summoned for Theo Butcher, manager of the Camden Operation and Paul Cooper from the Shreveport Operation to meet him in New Orleans. After a week of negotiations, a price was agreed upon, contracts were signed and the sale was finalized. Theo Butcher and Paul Cooper were paid a sizeable commission and they, along with his fleet of buyers, became employees of Delta Cotton Company.

John left Louisiana, heading for Attorney Benefield's office to report the transactions. The Red Cruiser left Baton Rouge on March 26, 1873. Four hours from port, *John died from an apparent heart attack. The boat docked at Alexandria and a telegram was sent to Benefield notifying him of the tragedy. He immediately went to the Crank's residence and notified them of John's death. Ben showed little emotion.*

"I'll return to the office and remove his "Last testimony" from the safe. Having read it, I will return so we can make plans as he requested."

It was revealed that his body was to be laid to rest at the Lambertine near his wife Ann and daughter Mary.

Benefield said, "I suggest that his body be shipped to Magnolia for preparations or if you wish we can have it brought here for preparations."

Elsie suggests "I think it would be simpler to ship him to Magnolia," Elsie interjected, 'What you think Ben?"

"Let's handle it in the simplest manner. Will we need to go to Magnolia and make arrangements?"

"We can if you want or mother and Alfred Marlar would be happy to act on our behalf."

"Let's ask the favor of them. When will the funeral be?"

"We'll have to wait and see. It will probably take at least a week or longer."

"The sooner the better." Ben then looked at Benefield and asked, "Can I read his Last Testament."

"I'm sorry Ben but it is privileged information. The judge and I are the only individuals to be burdened with the responsibility until probate, and that may be quite a while. You and I will discuss some of the items later so you will have a better understanding. You, being a minor, complicate things a bit."

John's body was shipped to Magnolia Arkansas for burial preparations. He was laid to rest at the Lambertine next to his wife, Ann and daughter Mary, on April 2, 1873.

In the morning of April 2, Dub, Elsie and Ben arrived at the funeral home at Magnolia around nine. Ben recognized a carriage parked out front as one belonging to the Lambertine. When they entered they saw Mrs. Effie and Railroad waiting for them. It was a very sad occasion but Ben was excited to see them, more especially Railroad. Ben and Railroad went into the viewing room and viewed the body. Railroad then returned to the door and motioned for the others to enter.

Shortly thereafter, the corpse was loaded into the hearse and the journey to the Lambertine began. Ben and Railroad followed the hearse in the Lambertine's carriage while Dub, Elsie and Mrs. Effie followed. They arrived at the Lambertine about noon and there were several carriages, wagons and horses parked around the home. Several of the local neighbors and some of the slaves had prepared a feast for the occasion. Many of John's business associates and all the slaves that remained in the area were present. The blacks had gathered at the back corner of the yard while the whites prepared their plates. After the whites were served they gathered on the front porch. Some sat on the steps and other sat on the edge of the porch, while a few of the elderly were sitting on chairs and benches the servants had supplied. Ben yelled to the blacks to come fix their plates. They remained as they were, unwilling to improperly dine with white folk present.

After a few minutes Ben said, "If you all will excuse me, I have friends in the back yard I would like to say Hello too." He then walked around the corner of the house and headed toward the congregation of slaves that had amassed.

"You all come get some food."

Big George replied, "Master Ben, it ain't proper. We'se waits til the white folks are done."

"Bull shit, y'all ain't slaves anymore. Come fix your plate." They reluctantly followed him to the food tables and, having made their plate, returned to the back corner of the yard. Ben sat on a chopping block and they gathered around him, asking questions. He saw Mississippi looking at him with a big smile on her face. He immediately recognized her.

"Mississippi, you have become a beautiful lady. You look a lot better than you did the day Roosevelt pulled you from Dourcheat Creek. You looked like a drowned rat."

"You talkin ' bout th day you pushed me in 'n- tried to drown me?"

"I didn't push you. You just slipped on the mud."

Laughing Railroad interjected, "Red River was the one that pushed you. He is not here, so we will blame him."

"Ain't done no such a thang, it wus Ben. Roosevelt never let me go fishin with yawl after that." Laughter spilled from the crowd.

"I wish I knew where Red River was, I would write him a letter," Ben responded.

"He couldn't read it." Mississippi said.

"If I were to write you, could you read it?"

"Maybe, Railroad has been trying to teach me but I ain't learning too fast. You write me and if I can't read it, he will read it to me." She looked at Ben with a big smile on her face and continued "Ben you ain't changed a bit. You looks like ye always did."

"Well, I can't say the same for you. You have made yourself out to be a beautiful woman. I can't believe you have grown so tall." Mississippi was about five-foot-ten, of, a very light complexion, a well developed body, straight auburn hair that was plaited into long pigtails on each side of her head and she had a beautiful smile that showed perfectly pearled teeth.

"I remember when we were kids, Red River, Railroad and I was always mean to you and made you cry."

"You shore did and you always called me 'Pick-a-ninny'. Red River, he done went to Louisiana with his mom and dad. Don't guess we will ever see him again. Y'all wus sure enough mean," she said with a big smile.

Ben was thinking out loud and embarrassed himself by saying "As beautiful as you are, I'll never be mean to you and make you cry again. I promise." Suddenly he felt his face becoming flushed. He expressed his thoughts in words too candidly not to be embarrassed. After they had eaten, Ben ordered, "Go get some dessert. There are several pies, cakes and a few cobblers. Let's go." Again there was reservation from the crowd that surrounded him.

"It ain't proper. We'll wait until the white folks are finished," Big George said.

"Bull shit; let's go before they eat it all". Ben headed for the dessert table and only a few followed.

After all had eaten, they walked to the cemetery, a few yards behind the house. They gathered around the grave site and Brother Evans said a few words before John was lowered into the ground. Some of the ex-slaves began to cover the casket. The crowd began to disburse. Some of the black women had built a fire under the wash pot for hot water for washing dishes. They had begun washing and drying dishes while the white women cleared the food from the tables.

"Alfred has asked us to spend the night," Elsie murmured to Dub." Do you want to and leave early in the morning or start home this afternoon? Regardless when we go, don't you quote scripture to Ben all the way back home!"

"I won't, and I don't care when we go back. Whatever Ben wants to do. Go ask him."

"Let's leave as soon as possible" Ben replied. Though he desired to spend more time with Mississippi, Ben reasoned: Maybe we can make it to Taylor by dark or shortly thereafter."

Ben went to the slave quarters and said good bye to his slave friends, making sure Mississippi was among them. He embraced her and whispered "I'll be back to see you, soon." A few minutes later, they had begun their return journey to Jefferson. Dub and Ben were riding in the front carriage seat and Elsie in the rear.

Ben remained shaken as the carriage continued along the road. Everyone was silent for a length of time. Finally Elsie glanced to find a smile on Ben's face.

She said, "Ben, you are smiling. What's the happy thought?"

"It was nice to see the slaves again, what few are remaining. I really enjoyed seeing Railroad and I have seen the most beautiful woman I ever laid eyes upon. Did you meet Mississippi?"

"Was she the tall 'high yellow' girl with pig tails?"

Ben turned in the seat to face her and said with a big smile on his face, "Isn't she beautiful? Too bad she is black, or else I wouldn't let her out of my sight."

Laughing Elsie said, "You would make a lot of girls at Jefferson unhappy if they knew you said that."

"There is not a girl in Jefferson that can compare to her and besides, they are all 'stuck-up'. She is definitely 'down to earth.' I hear up North that the white and black sometimes marry." Laughing he added "Maybe I should take her and head up there."

"Ben, you got to be kidding me."

"Only half kidding" he replied.

After arriving at home, Ben wrote both Railroad and Mississippi several letters. His only hindrance was Mississippi's illiteracy. Knowing Railroad would have to read her letters aloud, his esteem for was muddled and his words dulled.

CHAPTER 13

John's Will And Probate

The next week after John's death, Ben reported to the Law office as usual for his janitorial duties. Once the secretary had gone, Benefield called Ben into his office.

"Have a seat Ben; there are some things we need to discuss. You being a minor create a little problem. I think of you as being very mature, but what I think doesn't mean a hill of beans to the court." Ben sat very quietly, saying nothing. "Naturally your dad was your guardian. We now have two options. One is to make the Cranks your guardian and I have spoken to them about the matter, to which they have agreed. We can go to court and ask that your status be changed to an adult. I personally think that is the thing to do. Sometimes they agree and sometimes they will not consider it because of legal reasons. Regardless of which way it goes, you will need a personal attorney. I or no one from this firm wants to represent you but I can legally recommend anyone's service."

"Why will you not represent me?"

"I am not the type, but many attorneys take advantage of estate liquidations. I want you to have the peace of mind that you were treated fairly. You need someone to keep an eye on me," he said with a big smile. "Believe me; it will be better for both of us."

"I don't have any idea how to select an attorney."

"Ben, sometimes I'm very careless about leaving notes lying around. You may check the right front corner of my desk tomorrow and take a look at my housekeeping skills. If that is to be the case, and you happen to read the notes, don't tell me about it and leave them as they were. Your father's office has been locked since he left for New Orleans. No one has entered, but maybe you should do a little housekeeping just in case he left an open can of sardines in his desk drawer. Don't remove anything, "he said with a big smile, "Unless it's the sardines. His office key is placed in the second drawer down of my file cabinet, front right corner. Make sure you lock up. I'll see you in a couple of hours."

Benefield returned about eight thirty as Ben was finishing with the mopping.

"Are you about through? Elsie is probably waiting dinner for you."

"Yes, I have finished. Let us get out of here."

"You go ahead and I'll lock up. See you tomorrow afternoon."

The next afternoon as Ben came to the office, Benefield met him at the door.

"All you need is to dust the furniture. I'm going to the hotel if anyone needs me; I'll be back in a couple of hours."   Ben immediately went to dust Benefield's desk. Under a paper weight on the right corner of the desk, a few pieces of paper caught Ben's eye. Ben sat in Benefield's chair and retrieved the first note.

"Attorney: R. L. Boyette 416 Taylor Street, Magnolia Arkansas, a classmate of John Lewis at Baltimore School of Law. Has one son, Robert, age 17 who has enrolled at Baltimore School of Law, fall semester. Ben Lewis's tuition has also been paid for fall semester. R. L. Boyette handled sale of "Lambertine" to Alfred Marlar."

Ben sat in amazement and said to himself "What in the hell is he telling me? I can't believe Dad sold the Lambertine to Al. I guess that is why he moved here to Jefferson. What is this shit about "The Baltimore School of Law" and my tuition being paid? I guess he is telling me I need to meet Robert Boyette. Is this his recommendation to me to hire Attorney Boyette? What a shock! I don't know if I want to read the next."

The next note read:

"Sold: Lewis Cotton Company Shreveport, Lewis Cotton Company Camden and Lewis Cotton Company New Orleans to "Delta Cotton of New Orleans", Sale final. A substantial sum of money involved - payment awaiting verification of inventory. Proceeds were intended to finance constructions of M. O. & R.R. Railroad."

Ben sat for a while thinking about what he had just read. "Dad always wanted to be a railroad man rather than a cotton man. I wonder how substantial a sum this money amounts to?"

"You through with the cleaning?" Benefield asked as he entered the room.

"Yes, I'm finished." Ben said as he walked toward the door. He stopped, turned and said, "Thanks, Mr. Benefield".

The next week when Ben reported for work, Benefield asked that he come into his office. "Ben, I have business in Magnolia on Friday. Would you like to make the trip with me?

"Do you think I should?" he asked with hesitation.

"I most definitely do. We will return Sunday."

Smiling Ben said "Will we be back in time for church? If not, the preacher may not let me go."

"I have talked with them, there won't be a problem. I guess now you can get to work." Ben then started toward his broom.

September 23, 1874, three days after Ben's seventeenth birthday, Ben, the Cranks, Attorney Benefield and Attorney Boyette appeared before Judge J, D. West in "Texas Circuit Court." The purpose of the hearing was to deem Ben with the status of adult... After a lengthily court proceeding, Ben was classified as an adult with the exception of voting rights and the purchase of alcohol products.

Legal notices were posted that the "Last Will and Testament" of John Thomas Lewis would be probated January 10, 1875, ten o'clock a. m. Those present requested by the court were Benjamin Thomas Lewis, his attorney R. L. Boyette, Attorney J. H. Benefield, W. S. Crank, Elsie Crank, and Alford Marlar. There were also several spectators also in the court room. The judge called the court to order and stated, "This document has been recorded in the county records, volume 73, block A, page 1 through page 9 of Marion County Texas. All records have been notarized and witnessed by appropriate persons and filed by Marion County Clerk G. R. Foreman.

Last Will and Testament of John Thomas Lewis

Dated; November 10, 1871

I John Thomas Lewis of the County of Marion in the State of Texas knowing it is allotted that all men must die and being of sound and disposing mind and memory do make and publish this as my last will and testament revoking all others, therefore made by me.

First;

At my death I desire to be buried in a manner becoming my position and means. If these positions and means provide, I request to be laid by my wife "Ann" and child "Mary" at the "Lambertine

Plantation" 146 Military Road, Magnolia Arkansas, Columbia County state of Arkansas.

Second;

I desire all my past debts to be paid in as short a time as can be done with justice to my family conditions.

Third;

I give and bequest to my dear friend and servant, Alford Marlar, the property known as 'The Lambertine Plantation", including the home and furnishings, all farm equipment and animals and Land acreages as stated on deed.

Fourth;

I give and bequest to my dear friends W. S. and Elsie Crank, my bank account held by "The First National of Jefferson" known as "The Crank Account" and an additional five hundred dollars...

Fifth;

I give and bequest to my friend and attorney, J. H. Benefield the sum one thousand dollars.

Sixth;

I give and bequest to my dear friend, Mrs. Effie Martin, the sum of five hundred dollars.

Seventh;

I give and bequest to my son, Benjamin Thomas Lewis, My bank account held by "The First National Bank of Jefferson" known as "Baltimore School of Law," upon graduation from stated school. If requirement is not accomplished, the account shall be quested to Baltimore School of Law on December 31, 1880. Distribution of this account is to be made by Attorney J. H. Benefield.

Eight;

I give and bequest to Benjamin Thomas Lewis, all my remaining assets, including banking accounts held by "The First National of

Jefferson" and any other accounts that may be established after the date of this will and testament.

Signed; John Thomas Lewis

CHAPTER 14

College And Marriage

Ben graduated High School in May of 1875. He was one of the most popular students in High School. He was involved in the school athletics programs and academically, he was among the top of his class. Immediately after graduation Ben paid Benefield a visit.

"Why in the hell would dad force me to go to Maryland for school? I had rather go to the University of Texas. I have never been up north and I am not looking forward to it."

"I can't answer that, but I can tell you that your dad was an alumnus there. He had great hopes of Thomas becoming a lawyer but the war ended that dream. He has left you among the wealthiest men of Marion County, if not the wealthiest. I think you owe him as much. It is a very good school and you will lose a lot of money if you don't go. I have all the information you will need for enrollment and boarding. Rob Boyette has also enrolled there; I suggest you get acquainted with him; maybe you and he can room together. You don't have to decide now, he allowed ten years before the disbursement is to be made. If you know for sure you are not going and will sign a release, I can send the money to them now and close your dad's entire legal request

"I am moving to Magnolia and enrolling at Arkansas A & M for the summer session. That will give me all summer to decide." While living there he became friends with Rob Boyette. That fall, he and Robert enrolled in "The Baltimore School of Law."

During the next few years he and Robert had become very popular with the faculty and students. They lived in one of the most expensive apartments near campus and wore the most expensive clothing available. Their social life included extravagant parties with Baltimore's most wealthy. They had a classmate, Eugene DuPoint, who had become a very good friend. He invited them to his home for dinner. They accepted the invitation.

"Wonderful," Eugene replied. "Our carriage will pick you up at six- thirty, will that allow you enough time?"

"That will be fine, but we can rent a carriage and driver."

"Not necessary, there is no problem. You may dress casual, if you like. I'll see you'll tonight," he said as he walked away.

Rob asked "What are you wearing tonight?"

"I was thinking my western suit and cowboy boots. What do you think?"

"He said casual, so, I am thinking my overalls and a straw hat," Rob said laughing "But if you are going to dress as a cowboy, I will too."

They were waiting at the curb and a carriage arrived driven by a black man wearing a black formal suit and top hat. "Are you Mr. Lewis and Mr. Boyette?"

"Yes we are, Ben said. This is a mighty fancy carriage."

"My name is "Sam;" if you will please get in, I will drive you to the DuPoint Home."

They entered and looked at each other smiling. They were both thinking to themselves that Eugene dressed and acted like an ordinary student but they realized he must be of upper class. Near half an hour later, they were in a very influential neighborhood with large homes. When they neared a large rock archway the carriage entered the drive. The house, about two hundred yards from the street, was partially hidden by the large trees. Ben said in a low voice "What a mansion." The carriage circled a large flower garden and stopped near the entrance. As Ben and Rob were exiting the carriage, Eugene came from the house to greet them.

"Very nice home," Ben said.

"It serves the purpose quite well. I'm so pleased you came. My family is looking forward to meeting you. Want you come in."

They entered into a large entry. The house was as extravagant on the inside as the outside. Eugene directed them into a large living room. They saw a young girl reading a book. She appeared to be twelve or thirteen years old. After noticing the arrival of new guest, she put the book down and came toward them.

"This is my younger sister, Elizabeth. I have another up stairs, primping." As Elizabeth was shaking their hands and welcoming them, Mr. and Mrs. DuPoint entered. They were formally dressed and appeared to be in their late fifties or early sixties. Eugene made the introductions.

Mrs. DuPoint said "Gene has told us a lot about you. Which of you is from Arkansas?"

Rob replied "I am from Magnolia, actually we both are Arkies but Ben escaped to Texas."

Smiling, she to Ben, "I understand you are from east Texas."

"Yes ma'am. I was born in Arkansas but moved to Jefferson Texas at the age of eight."

A beautiful young lady entered. "This is my other sister, Marie," Eugene commented to the guests. "She is always the last here; she spends too much time primping."

"Now Gene, be nice and don't cause trouble," Mrs. DuPoint said, looking at Rob and Ben she added "he is always harassing her. Sometimes I just want to break his neck." They all laughed.

"Sorry to be late, you all seem to be having a good time."

Eugene said, "If you weren't always late, you would know why we are laughing."

"Gene, that's enough," Mrs. DuPoint scolded.

"I don't think I have met real cowboys before."

"I hope we don't tarnish your image," Ben replied to Marie.

The butler appeared and said, "Dinner is ready to be served."

They went into the dining room and Mr. DuPoint sat himself at the head of the table. Mrs. DuPoint sat adjacent to him.

"Ben would you and Rob please sit across from me. I'm anxious to get acquainted," Mrs. DuPoint requested. Rob sat across from her and Ben next to him. Elizabeth hurriedly took a chair next to Ben.

"Elizabeth, I will set next to Ben. You can set at the end."

"Why do I always have to set at the end, bossy?"

"Because, I said so."

"Now girls, stop fussing." Mr. DuPoint looked at Rob and Ben and added: "they are always at each other and their brother doesn't help matters."

"May I make a suggestion? May Marie set between Ben and me and I will set next to Elizabeth," Rob proposed. "I would like to watch her eat." They all laughed.

"Sure, I was hoping they wouldn't act child-like, but I should have known. They always do."

"It's not often that we have cowboys as dinner guest."

"The main course will be prime rib. I hope you will like it," Mrs. DuPoint said.

"Marvelous," Ben replied. He was hoping it wasn't lamb chops or something else he didn't care for.

They enjoyed a wonderful three course meal. The atmosphere was very relaxed and there was a lot of laughter, mostly caused by Mrs. DuPoint scolding Eugene and Marie for arguing. After dinner was complete Mrs. DuPoint asked, "Will your family be coming for the graduation ceremonies?

"Rob said, "My parents are so damn glad to get me out of school, they wouldn't miss it for the world." The question was then reflected towards Ben.

"I have no family. My parents have passed away. I had one brother and he was killed in the war. My only sister died of the fever before I was born. I lived with a family by the name of "Crank" but they will not attend. I do have a good friend, Railroad Dockery, who's more like a brother. We lived together for so long, until I moved to Jefferson."

"I'm sorry I asked. Railroad is a very unusual name. Will he attend?"

"No, I'm afraid we have lost contact. I haven't seen or heard from in about five years. I don't know where he is now."

They then retired to the living room and were having an enjoyable conversation when Ben noticed the time was almost ten o'clock. In his heavy southern draw he exclaimed "Lord of mercy, I didn't realize it was so late. I think Rob and I should make tracks." Mr. DuPoint went to summon Sam.

Ben's accent caught the attention of Marie, who sat next to him on the divan. "I love your southern accent. It is very charming. By the way, I have tickets for the Metropolitan Opera for next Saturday night. A girlfriend and I were going but her plans were disrupted. Would you like to accompany me?"

"Sure, I've never been to an opera."

"Sam and I will pick you up at seven o'clock."

Sam came to the door with their coats and cowboys hats. The boys bid everyone goodnight and entered the carriage where both could freely recount the evening's high points. Their conversation's remarks touched upon every detail of the evening.

"That was a fantastic meal, a hell of a lot better than the stew I was planning on. They seemed like nice people. Elizabeth and Marie were about to fight over who set next to you."

"Thanks for your solution. They were the down to earth type. I can tell Mr. DuPoint is richer than a yard up a bull's ass. When I saw the house, I figured they would be real uppity, but they weren't."

"It's appears that Marie has the hots for you, don't you think?"

Laughing Ben said "Don't they all?"

"You wish."

At the DuPoint household, Elizabeth yelled to her mother "Mother, Marie lied to Ben. She told him she had tickets to the opera and she doesn't have tickets." Her frustrated gaze then turned to Marie. "You made me mad when you wouldn't let me set next to Ben."

"I wanted to set next to my future husband and I will have opera tickets by Saturday night."

Laughing, Elizabeth replied, "You are too old for him and he has too much class for someone like you and I hope the opera has sold out."

"Little Miss Smarty Pants, you just wait and see."

Saturday evening the carriage arrived at Ben's door. "Well, Well! Look at you. Aren't you a gentleman?" Ben was wearing an expensive black suit, a stove type hat and he carried a cane.

"You don't look bad yourself. You didn't tell me what to wear; therefore I'm wearing my best. I didn't want you to be ashamed by the way I was dressed."

"As handsome as you are, you could wear whatever you like and I would be proud to be seen with you."

"Next time, I'll wear my overalls."

Rob was anxiously waiting for Ben's return. As Ben entered the door, Rob asked, "How was the date?"

"Sounded like a corral full of freshly castrated steers and the next minute it sounds like a pack of high-pitched hounds with a coon up a tree. A man has to go through a hell of a lot to get culture." Rob was rolling in the floor with laughter. "I'm going to the Symphony next week; I hope it is better than this opera."

After the symphony, Marie challenged Ben: "I have chosen the last two events. Would you like to plan the next?"

In his deep southern drawl he said, "Yep, let's go for a nice dinner and then go to the park and have sex on a picnic table."

She looked at him with a big smile and said, "Dinner sounds fine, but I will eat very slowly and I'm sure we will run out of time before the park. Besides, I'm afraid Sam would tell mother."

The next week, they had dinner at an exclusive restaurant. Ben wore his western suit and cowboy hat. He placed the hat in a vacant chair at their table. Shortly after being seated, Marie whispered, "There is a guy setting across the room that I know. His name is Butch. That's not his real name, but that is what we call him. He is a bully: arrogant and the most obnoxious person I have ever known. I hope he doesn't see me."

"Sounds like an old boyfriend to me."

"I had rather be dead than go out with him. His father and dad are business associates. He is always trying to start trouble."

As Butch and his party were leaving, he saw Marie and came to their table. "Hello Marie. I haven't seen you in quite some time."

"It has been a while," she responded, "though not long enough," she murmured to herself. "I would like for you to meet a friend, this is Ben Lewis."

Ben stood and shook his hand. "Pleased to meet you," Ben said and sat back down.

"Where did you come up with him? Butch asked Marie...He then looked at Ben and asked, "How did you get to town? With a herd of cattle?"

Very calmly Ben replied, "Believe it or not, I came on a boat. After you mentioned it, I haven't seen any cattle since arriving in Baltimore. But I know there is some around, otherwise where would you get the bull shit coming from your mouth?"

Butch's anger was interrupted by Marie: "Please, leave us alone, you obnoxious bastard."

"Sure." Butch moved toward the door, stopped, turned back and pointed his figure at Ben and adding, "Maybe we will meet again, cowboy."

"You had better hope not," Ben said.

"I'm sorry Ben. When I saw him I was afraid he would cause trouble."

"Don't give it a second thought. Let's hurry and eat and go to the park."

"She smiled and tried to talk with a southern accent saying, "Cowboy, we ain't goin to th park.""

On the night of May 30 1882, Eugene, Rob and Ben walked across the stage to receive their Diplomas. Afterward, a reception was held at "The Waterfront Hotel." Near the end of the event, after several drinks, Eugene and Rob each made a speech. Everyone began to clap and yell "Ben, Ben, Ben."

Ben went to the speaker stand and said, "A microphone makes me a little nervous but what I have to say really makes me even more nervous. I am going to omit the bull shit about how happy I am to receive this 'sheep skin.' It has been a long time coming and I am very elated. However, there is more important business than this diploma. Marie, would you join me up here?" She joined him at the speaker stand, not having any idea for the reason of his request. He went to one knee, took her hand and asked, "Marie, would you marry me?"

She was shocked into silence, then replied: "I would be happy to, I was afraid you would never ask."

Ben held up his hand to calm the applause. "I told you I was nervous and I forgot a very important formality." He then looked at Mr. DuPoint and said, "I am sorry; I have gotten things a little out of order. May I have your daughter's hand in marriage?"

"By all means, Mr. Lewis, please take her." The audience applauded and went to Marie and Ben with best wishes.

Rob was returning home and Ben informed Marie that he would be traveling with Rob. He had important business at Jefferson and he would return as soon as possible. When on the trip, Rob said to Ben, "Hell boy, you better run while you can."

Marie and Ben were married June 1, 1883. They had a very extravagant wedding and went to Europe for a month-long honeymoon. Upon returning, Mr. DuPoint insisted that Ben become a junior partner with his business. Ben accepted a position, but declined the junior partnership offer. He became very unpopular with his new family members. He and Marie resided in the spacious DuPoint Mansion with the family.

"I have an important announcement to make," Ben explained one December evening after dinner. The family became very quiet and gave him their attention. "Marie and I will soon be moving to Amarillo Texas."

"Like hell we will," Marie exclaimed after a short pause.

"Dear that is my plans. The city is growing at a rapid rate. I have discovered there is a great opportunity for someone interested in the banking business. I will be visiting there next week and I hope you will join me."

"I am not the least bit interested in joining you. I have plans to attend a D.A.R. Convention in Philadelphia next week."

"That's the first I've heard about it. It's your choice, Philadelphia or Amarillo."

Mr. DuPoint who had become very red-faced said "Young man that is the dumbest damn thing I have ever heard. Why in the hell would you go in search for opportunity when I have already made them available for you here?"

"Sir, with all respect, being from Texas, it has always been my desire to return. I prefer the open spaces to the congestion we have here. More importantly, I require my total independence."

Marie replied, "You may have total independence because I don't know if I will go."

"That is your choice, my dear but I hope you go with me and investigate."

"I have heard enough, please excuse me," Marie said as she

stormed from the room. Three days later she had her luggage packed for a trip to Amarillo.

CHAPTER 15

Move To Amarillo 1884

The next week Ben and Marie arrived in Amarillo and took residence in the Herring Hotel. After a month of touring, meeting and getting acquainted with some of the business people, Marie decided there was a possibility she would become pleased with the area. There was a large estate home for sale at 1101 Broadway Street which was located in the most influential part of town. Ben was interested: "Let's go look at the home."

Marie replied "I don't think it's wise to go shopping for a home now. We need to wait and see how we are going to like it here."

"I like here and this is where we will be living. After a while, if you don't like the house, we'll build what you want and sell this one, for a profit hopefully." They contacted the real estate company and purchased the ten-room home.

"My Dear, you have a big job to do. The home will need furnishing. Do you want to do it or do I need to hire an interior decorator?"

"I'll do it, Marie insisted."Do you think I'm going too sat on my butt and let you have all the fun?" Marie became busy shopping for furnishings. Amarillo had one small furniture store with a limited inventory. Most items had to be ordered from catalogs and shipped in. After a few days of frustration, Marie told Ben "while you are looking for a building for your bank, keep your eyes open for a building suitable for a furniture store. I'm going into the furniture business."

"Do you know anything about the furniture business?"

"Probably as much as you know about banking, which is very little. I have family members who own "Peck & Gregory" in Chicago. They are the largest wholesaler distributor in the United States. I will hire someone from that firm to manage it. We will keep our business ventures separate and when you lose your ass, maybe I will loan you enough to keep you a-float," she said with a smile.

Over the next few weeks, Ben was busy acquiring real estate and locating an architect and contractor to build "The First Commerce Bank of Amarillo."

Marie returned to Baltimore to visit family and friends. She also visited Peck & Gregory in Chicago, shopping for furniture. She had a first cousin working there and she asked if he would like to manage a furniture store in Amarillo, Texas. He was not happy working in the family owned business and he told her he would love to live and work in Amarillo. She hired him as her store manager. She told him to decide on an inventory list. The store would contain approximately 10,000 square feet.

"How much are you willing to invest in inventory?" he asked.

"You are the manager, just remember this is Texas. Moderate class, nothing real fancy. Review your past sales going to Texas and decide for yourself." Laughing she added, "It will be your neck on the chopping block if you screw up. The building should be completed in a few months. Have the shipment ready and I will notify you when to ship. You will need to arrive before the inventory and decide on floor layout." Three weeks later her home purchases were arriving at the depot.

A 10,000 square foot building was under construction which was to become "The Marie Lewis Furniture Company". By 1885 the furniture store was completely stocked and in full operation.

Marie had been busy meeting the ladies of Amarillo and forming a Chapter of the D.A.R. She visited a Mrs. Colsen who lived on a ranch west of town. The reason for the visit was to interest her in the D.A.R. meeting. Mrs. Colsen's husband had died eight years prior and she had listed the ranch with a real estate company for sale. Marie inquired about the property and became interest in the purchase.

When Ben returned home that afternoon, Marie met him at the door and said "Cowboy, what do you know about ranching?"

"Not a whole lot except that is where bull shit is produced. Why do you ask?"

"I'm thinking about buying the Colden Ranch."

"You have to be kidding, are you out of your mind? Why would you want to a do a foolish thing like that?"

"I had rather be referred to as "The lady who owns a ranch west of town" rather than the yankee woman from Baltimore."

"You're serious, aren't you?

"Hell yes I'm serious. I need to buy some western cloths and learn to ride a horse. I have an appointment with Cody Cutting, the ranch overseer, to teach me to ride."

"Marie, ranching is a touch business. You need to know what you're doing to make money."

"Who said anything about making money? I just want to be

known as a ranch owner. Cody knows what he is doing and he has agreed to manage it. I have my own money and I'm going to purchase it." Three months later Marie was the proud owner of a twenty-five hundred acre ranch know as the "The Marie Lewis Cattle Company."

The Lewis Family had become very popular among the business people and was receiving invitation to many social events. This was very exciting to Marie because of her desire to become a socialite. She volunteered to serve on any civil committee that was made available to her.

Within five years, not only was The First Commerce Bank in operation, but Ben had opened a small branch bank in Channing Texas. He had purchased "The C & L Coal Company of Brownwood Texas," and was also serving as president of "West Texas Telephone Company."

Marie had become very active with the Daughters of The American Revolution (D.A.R's) and traveled frequently, speaking and forming new chapters of the D.A.R. In 1885 she became pregnant and was very unhappy due to the interruptions in her social life. She gave birth to a daughter "Sarah" on January 12, 1886. Sara was cared for by a governess and Marie continued her travels.

CHAPTER 16

Sarah's Childhood 1898

On one of Marie's return visits to Amarillo, she told Ben she was going to send Sarah a boarding school in Baltimore. Ben objected, "Why don't you let the child have a normal life?"

"She can't have a normal life in this god damn cow town. The schools are inadequate and she is probably already behind the girls in boarding school. I don't want her growing up thinking horseback riding is high class activity and I sure don't want her marrying a tobacco chewing cowboy."

"You married a cowboy and you didn't think anything was wrong with that. She is happy here and has her friends and besides that, I want her here with me."

"If you want to be with her, you better pack your bags because you will be moving to Baltimore along with her.

"Marie, she is only twelve years old. Let her finish high school and then send her to some high class college."

"She will be going to Mary Sharp College in Murfreesboro Tennessee."

"Hell, Marie, don't make every decision for the child. Give her some freedom and independence, and let her decide on a few things herself."

"Sometimes parent have to help with these decisions. No telling where you would be today if your dad hadn't insisted you go to Baltimore."

Ben was usually very calm, seldom used profanity and rarely raised his voice but her remark infuriated him. "You bitch. You had better get the hell out of my sight."

"I can't believe you just called me a bitch."

In a calm voice Ben replied, "I'm sorry, but sometimes I call it the way I see it." Marie avoided contact with him for a few days as she was packing Sarah's belongings for the move. The following week, Sarah, her governess, Marie and her private maid Ophelia, boarded a train to Baltimore.

At age 17 in 1903, Sarah enrolled in "Mary Sharp College" located in Murfreesboro Tennessee. It was Marie's Alma Mater. She became pregnant at age 18. Marie was very upset and became very irritate.

"What would everyone think if they knew I had a whore for a daughter and a bastard for a grandchild?" She forced Sarah to move to Jasper Tx., a small town in East Texas, and was not allowed to return to Amarillo until after the child was born and adopted. Marie was present on October 27, 1904 when the child was born. She made sure Sarah never saw the child. Ben was not in total agreement with Marie over her decisions. She told him "Ben, I saw the child and adoption is the best thing. He was not fully developed. His left hand had a normal thumb, large and index finger, but the two small fingers were about half as long as normal. No telling what other problems he may have. We know nothing of his father. He is probably from some common family. Believe me, adoption is best." Ben made no comment and asked no questions.

Sarah returned to school at Mary Sharp College and graduated in 1906. She then returned to Amarillo.

Marie's father died in Baltimore and the Lewis Family traveled to the funeral. Ben returned to Amarillo the following week but Marie and Sarah remained there for a few months. During this time Marie was busy doing "match making" parties and inviting the friends with relatives of eligible bachelors. Sarah was introduced to Dr. John McCormick who was doing his intern at Baltimore's Saint Michael Hospital. Marie returned home, insisting that Sarah stay and continue to visit with relatives. Sarah remained there for another few months. Marie received a telegram that Dr. McCormick had proposed to Sarah.

Marie began immediately making arrangements for a large wedding to set in Amarillo. John and Sarah wanted to be married in Baltimore but Marie would not hear of it. She demanded that Amarillo host the wedding. John was having second thoughts about the marriage, after learning of the demanding ways of Marie. He was quite concerned about the influence she would have on Sarah and withdrew the proposal. Sarah returned to Amarillo. The pair continued to be in close contact, writing to each other almost daily. John came to Amarillo and re-proposed and agreed to be married Amarillo.

CHAPTER 17

Sarah's Wedding 1907

The wedding date was set for Saturday, May 30 1907. Wednesday afternoon, Ben had an appointment with the tailor for the finial fitting of his tux. He was hurriedly trying to complete his business for the day.

A black man came into the bank and asked to see Mr. Lewis. Mary Smith, Mr. Lewis' secretary asked if he had an appointment. He replied "No ma'am didn't think I would need one."

"Mr. Lewis is very busy and will not be able to see you today. If you would like to make an appointment, I will schedule for you to see him tomorrow. What is the nature of business?"

"We don't have business, we're old friends"

"What is your name and I will tell him you are here."

"My name is Railroad Dockery."

Mary went into Ben's office "There is a black man who wants to see you," she told him. "I told him I would make him an appointment but he said you were friends. His name is Railroad Dockery."

Ben had a surprised look on his face and repeated the name. "Railroad Dockery?" He rushed to the bank lobby. The two men both began laughing and rushed to each other. They did not shake hands but embraced each other with affection. Ben's employees stared at him as he hugged this black man, which was out of character for him. He took notice and explained, "This is my brother, Railroad. We would lay on his mother's chest, him sucking the tit on the left while I sucked the one on the right. We would look at each other and wonder if we looked like each other." He and Railroad had a big laugh and Ben motioned for him to follow him into his office. He turned to Mary as he closed the door behind them and said, "Don't disturb us; we have a lot of catching up to do."

Mary looked at the tellers and said "I don't believe what I just saw and heard. Did you hear him say he had sucked a black tit? That is not at all like him to say something like that." They all had a good laugh.

Ben asks, "What have you been doing for so many years?" Ben hesitated, calculating the years, "I haven't seen you in over twenty years."

Railroad told him that after the Lambertine closed, he moved into a cabin on Mrs. Effie's place. "She encourages me to continue to draw. She insisted that I go to Magnolia and take oil painting lessons. The lady who was instructing, at first didn't want me in her class because I was black. I showed her some of my drawings and she agreed to instruct me. After a while they began to build the railroad through Columbia County. It is three miles south of the Lambertine at a place called Waldo. They didn't use the survey your dad had laid out; it would cost too much to cross Dourcheat Bottom. The town was being laid out and the first building being build was "The First National Bank." They were almost complete with the building when

Mrs. Effie told me we were going to Waldo. She told me to draw a picture of the building and then draw several images of the front door and windows. On each of these drawings, I drew and painted the name in different fonts and added an assortment of colors. Mrs. Effie and I visited the contractor and asked if I could paint the door and windows. They were impressed with my work and asked what I would charge. Before I was able to come up with a price, Mrs. Effie said "It will be free, No charge." They agreed and selected the window painting they wanted from my drawings. On the way home Mrs. Effie explained, "You do the first job for free and charge for the rest." As Waldo developed, I painted window signs in all of the buildings and later painted advertisements on the buildings sides. I was Waldo's Sign Painter for several years and I painted a few portraits too."

When the railroad crew reached Waldo, I went to work for the railroad. After a few days, they realized I had a little education and gave me a job as a clerk. The office was a railroad car that moved with the construction site. The foreman was a black man from St Louis and his daughter, Margie, also worked in the office. She and I married at Lewisville Arkansas on April 25, 1886."

Ben interrupted, "Did you jump the broom handle the way the slaves would marry, or did you get a preacher?"

Laughing, Railroad said "We did it like the white people, we got a preacher." He then continued, "By the time the track reached Texarkana, she was pregnant. She went to St. Louis to stay with her mother until the child was born. When the construction job was complete, I went to St. Louis to join her. I did odd jobs and painted whenever I could. I later joined the railroad crew again. We were re-building track from Texarkana to Vernon, Texas. We just completed the job and I decided to visit you before returning to St. Louis."

"I'm sure glad you did. I have often wondered what happened to you".

There was a knock on the door, "Mr. Lewis, I know you said not to disturb you, but have you forgot about the tailor?"

"No, thank you Mary, we are leaving."

After a few minutes they emerged from the office. As they walked out the door, Ben said, "Railroad and I are going to see the tailor."

The tailor not only made a finial fitting to Ben's tux, but measured Railroad for a very expensive black suit and white shirt. They purchased a red tie and a pair of black, expensive shoes. Railroad never dreamed he would be dressed so handsomely. The tailor promised Railroad's suit would be ready Friday afternoon. They then went to another store and Ben purchased him a set of more casual clothes and shoes.

Ben was later arriving at home that afternoon and Marie sat waiting. She had called the bank to inquire why he was running late and was told of Railroad's visit. Ben could see the anger on her face as he and Railroad entered. Marie asked Railroad to wait outside. He stepped out and closed the door behind him.

"Have you lost your god damn mind?" Marie asks in a very loud voice. "What was the idea of telling Mary and the tellers that you have a nigger for a brother and you sucked a nigger's tit?"

"Well, Marie, it is the truth and I am not one bit ashamed of it. That's the way it was."

"What do you plan to do with the nigger?"

"Don't call him a nigger. His name is Railroad and that is what I expect you to call him."

"What in the hell are you going to do with him?"

"Put him up in one of the guest bedrooms."

"Like hell you are! The governor and Mrs. Lanham will be using a guest bedroom. They would not like a nigger in the next room. I suggest you send his black ass back to Arkansas where he came from."

"That will never happen," Ben said, realizing it was better not to press the issue. "He can room with Felix. I'll show him his new living quarters."

"God damn you Ben. If this stupid act of yours makes the gossip section of the newspaper, I'll never forgive you."

"Marie, I personally don't give a shit if it does, or not. Take this as a warning. Under no circumstance, will you mistreat Railroad, and I mean what I say."

"Don't you threaten me or you will be rooming with him and Felix, and just when did you get into a position to tell me what to do?"

"When I became majority owner of the Amarillo Newspaper. I just may submit an article for the gossip column myself, if you continue to raise hell," he said, as he turn and went outside to Railroad. They then went to the servants' quarters and Ben introduced Railroad to Felix. "Railroad will be helping you get ready for the wedding."

The next morning Ben summoned Railroad to meet him for breakfast. Marie would have no part of joining them. Blacks were not allowed to eat with whites. During the day Railroad and Felix were busy mowing the lawn, trimming hedges, washing windows and many other choirs preparing for the weekend.

Friday was a busy day, with tents being erected on the lawn. Lawn chairs were delivered and stored for use the next day. Railroad and Felix made a trip to the railroad depot to pick up a train car load of flowers that Marie had ordered from "Furrow & Co. Floweriest" in Guthrie Oklahoma. She was present checking the flowers as they were unloaded and shouting orders to Railroad and Felix. Later that day Railroad and Ben went to the tailor for his finial fitting of his suit. Later in the afternoon, Railroad and Felix went to one of Marie's friend to get a covered carriage and horses to use along with theirs for the big event. They were to meet the train and Felix was to escort Governor and Mrs. Lanham to the residence and then return to the depot. He and Railroad were to take other dignitaries from the depot to the Executive Suites of The Herring Hotel.

The hotel's main dining room was set up to serve dinner to approximately two hundred guests. Some of the regular guests were seated and the dignitaries were to arrive later and be introduced to the audience. Ben and Marie were standing at the top of the stairway. Marie called attention and addressed the audience. "I would like to introduce to you: the bride and groom, Miss Sarah Lewis and Doctor John McCormick." They appeared at the top of the stairs, waved to the audience and descended the stairs. Next to be introduced were "The Honorable Governor of Texas, "Governor Samuel Willis Lanham and his lovely wife Oveta Lanham". They entered to top of the stairs, waved to the audience and then descended the stairs, Followed by, "The honorable Ernest O. Thompson, Mayor of Amarillo and his lovely wife May Peterson Thompson." Several Chairwomen of D. A. R. chapters were introduced. The list continued. A few more couples arrived before the guest list had all been introduced. As Marie was starting to descend the stairs to join the guest, Ben held up his hand and said, "I have one more guest I would like to introduce. This is one of my very best friends. I have known him all my life. I would like to introduce to you, Railroad Dockery." Railroad appeared at the top of the stairs in his new formal dress with a big smile on his face and he waved to the audience. The room became very quiet, Marie looked as if she was going to faint. Ben escorted Marie to their seats, followed by Railroad who was seated next to Ben. During this time period, Negros was not allowed to eat in "white establishments".

Saturday morning shortly after sunrise, Felix and Railroad were busy setting up chairs, placing flowers as directed, rolling out a white carpet runner and preparing for the afternoon wedding. After lunch they were busy driving the carriages to the Herrington Hotel and bringing the wedding guest.

After the wedding, appetizers and champagne was served. Later a buffet dinner was served, catered by the chiefs of the Herrington Hotel. Railroad and Felix were busy returning the guest to the Hotel or railroad depot.

Sarah and John traveled to Europe for their honeymoon. They were to return in two months. During this time, Marie had purchased a nice house at the corner of Main and Oak Street. She was preparing a home for them and she had arranged for office space for John's practice. When they returned, they were both upset that Marie intended to be that demanding. John informed her that he would be practicing medicine in Baltimore. And they would be traveling there next week. Marie, with a very disappointed look on her face, turned and ran up the stairs. After a few minutes, Sarah told John "I'll go see if I can calm her down."

Sarah went to Marie's room and knocked on the door and entered. Marie was setting on the bed crying. "After all I've done for you and you treat me this way. I have spent a lot money and time finding you a place to live. I am almost through furnishing the house, about all I like to do is stock the pantry. I have even found John a good location for his practice."

Sarah stood quietly until Marie had spoken her peace then she said, "Mother, you should have spoken to us about all of this. I love you but you are not going to control our lives. John will not stand for it nor will I. We are leaving Friday for Baltimore and that is where we will live. John broke off the engagement because of you and you are not going to destroy our marriage. I hate to sound rude, but the sooner you realize this, the better it will be for all of us." Sarah turned and walked out as Marie began to cry. Marie stayed in her room the rest of the day.

The next morning, Marie summoned Ofelia, her personal maid and gave her a piece of paper. "Pack my trunk with these items. You and I are taking a trip. We may be gone for quite a while". Later that morning she left without saying a word to anyone. She went to Baxter Reality and listed the house she had bought for Sarah and John. She returned later that afternoon and told Ben "I almost forgot to tell you, but I have been invited to speak at the D.A.R. convention in Memphis next week. Now that I will be available, I will attend." She handed him a piece of paper reading "76 Front Street Memphis Tennessee." "That will be my address. Please have my mail forwarded." She avoided the rest of the family that night as she was busy packing and addressing post cards to her friends with her address in Memphis.

The next morning she summoned Felix to take her, Ophelia and her baggage to the train depot. She spoke very briefly to Sarah and John as she was leaving. "Please don't forget us here in Amarillo and please come back for a visit as soon as possible."

Ben contacted Baxter Reality and purchased the house at Oak and Main for rental property.

Railroad visited for another month and planned to return to St. Louis to be with his family. Ben asked if he would be interested in moving to Amarillo. "I would like too, but I don't think the wife would agree," he replied.

"If you ever decide, I will have a house for you. We will find you an art studio and you can paint signs here. If that isn't enough to keep you busy, we'll find you something else."

"I will try to talk my wife into it. Maybe she can get a teacher's job at the Negro School."

"Talk her into it. I would love you living here," Ben said as they shook hands. Felix was waiting with the carriage to take Railroad him to the depot.

As Railroad was walking to the carriage he turned and said, "If I decide to move here, Mrs. Marie is not going to be happy."

Ben laughed and said, "Who gives a shit. She is not around much anyway" as he turned and walked toward the house.

CHAPTER 18

Amarillo Beautification 1907

Marie returned home from Memphis two months later. After she was home for a while, Ben said "You had a message from Baxter Reality. They have a check waiting for you."

"Oh good, they must have sold my house. I wonder who bought it."

"I did."

"Like hell you did. I won't sell it to you."

"You don't have a choice, it's a done deal. I have power of attorney to sign your name during you absence and you were absent."

"What in the hell do you plan to do with it, rent it?"

"Already have, the new residents will be moving in shortly."

"Who did you lease too?"

"I have rented it to a man and woman by the name of 'Railroad and Margie Dockery.'"

Marie became furious. Her face became very red and in a trembling voice she shouted "You son of a bitch, you have lost your god damn mind? There will not be any niggers living in my house and besides that, the citizens of Amarillo will not allow niggers living within the city limits."

"In the first place, it's not your house. Second place, they are not niggers, they are black people. If the citizens don't like it, they can move the god damn city limits to exclude Oak and Main Street. I don't give a shit how pissed off you are, this is going to happen." He then turned and walked away.

A few days later, she was waiting for Ben at the door when he came from work. "What in the hell is this talk of you getting involved in the garbage business? I understand that you spoke at city the council meeting about the trash and garbage in Amarillo."

"That I did. The city is not taking good care of the situation. The garbage is not being picked up on a regular basis and many residents are dumping trash on any vacant lot they see. I have five lots on the south side that rubbish is piled up four feet deep. I have thirty acres of un-developed land by the river that is nothing but a trash pile. I'm tired of having to pay to keep my properties clean. It's time the city does something. What garbage they do gather is being pied in a field on the south side of town. The city development is moving that way and in a few years that area of town is going to be a mess. What the city needs is a landfill out of town. There is a canyon about two miles out of town on the west side that would make a good landfill."

"You're not talking about my ranch are you?"

"Yes I am. I didn't tell them you owned the property."

"You and your city council can go to hell. There is no way they are going to dump on my land."

"You were a big contributor to the library and hoped that they would name it after you. If you donated the canyon they may name it "The Marie Lewis Garbage Dump" he said with a smile. She became furious and said, "I don't want the name "Lewis" associated with Amarillo trash and garbage. My advice to you is to keep your damn nose out of it and let someone else handle the problem. You need to spend your time running the banking business and try to keep the bills paid."

"I'm not having any problems paying the bills." Ofelia came to the door and informed them dinner would be served when they were ready.

"Serve him, I'm not hungry," Marie ordered as she stormed up the stairs.

The next day Mayor Thompson called "Marie, welcome home. I hope you had a pleasant trip."

"Thank you, Mayor. I have been very busy traveling through the United States helping to form chapters of the D.A.R. It is a slow process, but we are making some headway. I will soon be spending time on the west coast."

"God bless you for your efforts. This world needs more women like you. If I may, I would like to get to my reason for the call."

"Sure, how may I be of help?'"

"The city is forming a committee to get involved in a "Beautification Program" for the city. I would like to ask if you would be interested in serving the on committee."

"I certainly would. Ben and I have spoken several times about the rubbish that is accumulating on the vacant properties throughout the town. I have visited many cities and it appears to me that it is time we do something."

"The city council will meet Tuesday night, would you like to address the council and express your views."

"Yes I would, please place me on the agenda. I will be there."

"Thank you so much, I knew we could count on you."

She met Ben at the door as he came home. "The mayor called and asked if I would serve on an "A Beautification Committee".

"Did you tell him to go to hell? I didn't think you were going to get involved in the garbage problem."

"The Mayor asked me. You know I couldn't refuse his request. He is aware of my influence on the people and it wouldn't do anything but increase my popularity. I will address the council on Tuesday night. Do you plan to attend?"

Laughing Ben said "I wouldn't miss it for the world."

Marie addressed the council with a lengthily speech and informed them of the many cities she had visited, Amarillo's downtown cleanliness was below standards in comparison. She volunteered to serve on the committee and suggested that the council accept a donation of forty acres of land that she owned on the west side of town for a new landfill. Ben was laughing to himself about the way she had changed views after getting into the spot light.

Marie contacted many cities inquiring about their sanitation departments and their means of handling refuse. She prepared a program and presented it to the council. It would require hiring several employees to be supervised by the Public Works Department. Ben objected and suggested that a contract be issued for an independent contractor to handle the problem. The residents would be charged a monthly fee to support the expense. The city works department and city attorneys created a contract and it was released and posted for bid proposals.

Marie had made temporary residence at Charleston S. C. for the next two months. She and other regencies of the D.A.R. were having a convention to organize chapters in Georgia, South Carolina, and North Carolina.

When she returned home, she was informed that the city had

awarded a contract. The contract was awarded to Railroad Dockery, owner of "Dockery Salvage." Marie became furious as she realized that Ben had maneuvered her into the donation of the property, but most important he had formed a company for his good friend.

Railroad had purchased property near the city dump and had acquired the necessary equipment and hired employees to provide trash removal two days a week from the entire city.

After a few weeks Marie informed Ben she and Ophelia would be spending time in Santa Fe. Her address would be the LaFonda Hotel. "If you like, you and your damn nigger can live together and sleep in the same bed as you did when you were kids."

"I don't think his wife would approve. I don't know if I could sleep with someone in the same bed with me. I have got use to sleeping alone since you chose your private bedroom several years ago. I don't think things will be a hell of a lot different, you in Santa Fe or wherever. You spend more time away than you are at home. Feel free to call or come home anytime you would like.

The Amarillo Press headlines the next day read;

"AMARILLO TO GET PARK, Twenty five acres of land along the Canadian River has been donated to the city for use as a park. The park will be named "The Marie Lewis Park."

Felix had loaded Marie's belongings into the carriage, as they were leaving for the depot, Ben came from the house. Marie said to him, "I have seen the morning paper: Thanks for the park."

With a big smile he said, "The least I could do after they didn't name the city dump after you."

CHAPTER 19

Marie Dies

June 20, 1910, Ben received a letter from Marie.

Dear Ben.

Ophelia and I will arrive on the Friday P. M. train. Please notify Felix to be waiting. I have planned a tea for two o'clock Saturday afternoon for approximately thirty ladies. Have Felix clean and do yard work according. The chief of the Herring Hotel will set up tables and provide refreshments. Mary has taken care of the guest list and invitations.

See you Friday

Marie

When Marie arrived home, Ben met her at the door. When she entered the Fourier; she saw a 24 x36 inch portrait of her and Ben on an easel. She immediately went to investigate. "Where in the world did you get this? I have never seen a portrait of such quality."

"It was a gift. The artist signed the lower right corner."

She put on her glasses and leaned in to read the signature.

She then looked at Ben with a surprised look on her face and said "Railroad Dockery? Did he paint this? I had heard that he painted but I had no idea he was capable of this." She stood, admiring the painting for several minutes and then said, "My hands look too fat."

Ben laughed, "They look natural to me." He was expecting some negative comment.

Saturday afternoon the ladies had gathered in front of the painting, admiring the precise details and quality of work.

"Marie who is this artist, Railroad Dockery?"

"He is one of our very best friends. He and Ben have known each other all their life. We had asked him and his wife many times to join us here in Amarillo and after years of persuading they agree. He has an art studio on highway 287 and he is responsible for keeping our city clean. He and his wife, Margie, are black but educated and very respectful. She teaches at the black school."

After receiving the portrait, Marie then began to call him Mr. Dockery. She often visited his studio and referred many customers to him.

Over the next twenty years, Marie traveled through the United States in support of The Daughters of The American Revolution. Her travels would take her away from Amarillo for several months at a time. She had established addresses at the following cities Los Angles Ca., New Orleans La., Santa Fe N.M., San Antonio TX, Dallas Tx., Washington D.C., Charleston S.C. and various other cities throughout the United States.

In 1913, she campaigned successfully for the "West Texas Regency of D.A.R." At the onset of the war in 1917, she appeared before the U. S. Congress and became instrumental in establishing programs such as the "Veterans Dependents Relief Fund," local chapters of "The American Red Cross" and other programs for the benefit of war veterans.

In 1920, she was nominated and ran for the "National President of D.A.R" Unfortunately, after campaigning extensively for several months she was defeated in the national election.

June 1, 1929 shortly after speaking at a D.A.R. Convention in Ft. Worth TX, she collapsed and was rushed to Harris Hospital. Ophelia notified Ben of her illness. He and Railroad left immediately for Forth Worth. They arrived seven hours later. Unfortunately she died within three hours of collapsing. Her death was ruled as an apparent heart attack.

Ben handled the necessary requirements and hired a funeral home to transport her body to Amarillo for preparations.

The news of her death was carried in many local, state and national newspapers.

She was laid to rest in Pioneer Rest Cemetery on June 11, 1929 at 74 years of age.

Marie had always enjoyed expensive jewelry. After the funeral, Ben told Sarah to take all of her jewelry and any other items of value she wanted. Sarah and John returned to Baltimore the following week.

CHAPTER 20

Bank Crash

The Wall Street Crash of October 24, 1929 was the beginning of the Great Depression. On that day stock prices began to fall and they continued to fall, at an unprecedented rate, for a full month. At the time of the crash most industrial production, for the most part, was in a healthy and balanced condition. Within weeks, large banks that were invested heavily in the stock market had seen their balance sheet values drop at an extremely fast rate. Large manufacturing companies had seen their stock values plummet and operating capital had become impossible to obtain. Due to shortage of capital, they were unable to order necessary supplies and make payroll. Many companies were forced into large layoffs and later bankruptcy. The Great Depression had begun.

As news of the banks closings spread, a national financial panic began. Depositors rushed to the banks to close their accounts and collect cash. Within a few hours of the run, banks were locking customers out because liquid cash had been exhausted.

The First Commerce Bank of Amarillo experienced the usual customer panic. Ben tried to calm his customers and requested that they demand a partial withdrawal, yet, very few agreed. He was forced to close the doors. He placed a sign on the door reading, "Bank Closed for One Week."

The largest depositor with assets that could become liquid was his late wife, Marie. Her largest account carried as "Marie Lewis DuPoint" had assets of over sixty thousand dollars, left to her by her father. She had intended to change the account to "Marie Lewis DuPoint" or "Sarah McCormick," but the account name was never changed. There were Federal Certificates of Deposit that had passed maturity dates, having a value of forty thousand dollars. Ben had the "Power of Attorney" on Marie's behalf until her death. This account now belongs to Sarah after Marie's death, but no legal transfer had been taken place. Ben issued notes from the First Commerce Bank, payable to Sarah McCormick for replacement of the Federal Notes. Ben made a trip to the Federal Reserve Bank in Dallas and redeemed the notes. Wells Fargo was paid to deliver the cash to the bank within five days. A few days later an agent with Wells Fargo entered the bank carrying a bag containing the cash. The money was counted and Ben signed the receipt. He immediately placed a sign on the door reading, "BANK NOW OPEN---CASH AVAILABLE. Within a few hours customers were lined up to make withdrawals.

The rush appeared to be over and Ben had begun to feel the bank would be able to survive, although it had an extremely low amount of liquid cash. The local area had been suffering an extreme drought for two years. Farm production was at an unusual low level and ranchers were disposing of their cattle due to grass shortage. Many of the creditors were unable to make mortgage payments and moved away seeking employment.

March 10, 1930, Mary, Ben's secretary said, "Ben, your daughter, Sarah is on the phone."

Ben hurriedly answered the phone, "Hello Sarah, what a pleasant surprise. It's great to hear your voice."

"Hi Dad, how are you?"

"I'm doing well. How are you? Your voice is very clear; sounds like you are next door."

"Actually, I'm here in Amarillo."

"Are you at the depot? I'll be right there and get you."

"No, I'm at the Herrington Hotel."

"What are you doing there? You will be staying with me, won't you?"

"No, I'll be staying here for a couple of days. I didn't notify you I was coming and didn't want to impose. You will meet me here tonight for dinner, won't you?"

"Of course, why don't you come to the house for dinner?"

"No, that will be too much trouble. Can you meet me here at seven o'clock?"

"Of course, I'll be there. I am looking forward to seeing you. See you then."

She said, "O.K. Bye" and hung up.

Ben sensed that Sarah was acting unlike herself... He was very puzzled by her strange actions. He began to wonder why she would not notify him she was coming and why she would not stay at the house. He had not seen her since Marie's funeral eight months ago, and he had received only one letter.

They met at the Harrington and enjoyed a nice dinner. She told Ben all about their new home in an exclusive addition called "Oak Hurst" about ten miles from downtown Baltimore. The house was a large four bedroom located on a large waterfront property. John's medical practice was doing quite well. The only problem was that he has to work too many hours.

"I have great news. I am about to become a grandmother and you a great grandfather. Charlene and Robert are expecting in July. He is a petroleum engineer and his company is transferring him to Tulsa Oklahoma. That just makes me sick. I tried to talk him into changing jobs where they could remain in Baltimore but jobs are hard to find. You would not believe the unemployment in Baltimore."

"Yes I would, it's the same here and possibly worse."

"I can't believe she would allow him to her move away."

"Mothers don't want their birds to leave the nest. Remember how upset Marie got when you moved to Baltimore. There is nothing you can do, let them be free and do their thing."

"I know there is nothing I can do, but I don't have to like it."

Laughing, Ben said, "You sound just like your mother." He did not realize she was so much like Marie. He could see her domineering features.

"They will be moving in a few weeks. Robert is already there and has found them a home. I wish she would stay until after the baby is born but she is looking forward to moving."

"That will give you something to do in your spare time. You can visit often."

"I may purchase a home there and live there a few months of the year."

"You really sound like your mother, now." He then became aware that his remarks were annoying her.

They visited until about ten o'clock and Ben said, "I soon need to go. I know it has been a long day for you, but you will come by the bank when you get up and start moving around, won't you."

"Sure, I will be there about ten o'clock."

'I'll go now and will be looking forward to seeing you in the morning." They embraced and Ben left.

The next morning Sarah and two professionally men entered the bank. Ben was surprised to see them. He met them shortly after they entered. Sarah's greeting was not very cordial. "Hi, Dad. This is Thurman Clark, John and my attorney. And this is Neal Stearns with the Potomac Bank of Baltimore."

Ben looked at them not really knowing what was taking place. He said, "What can I do for you?"

"John and I have discussed our situation and believe it in our best interest to transfer my account to Potomac Bank in Baltimore."

"Sarah, I can't believe you would consider such a thing. Your mother's account is the largest individual account this bank holds. I can't afford to lose it. With the recent problems I have had, surely you can't be serious."

"The recent banking problems are the reason we decided to make the transfer. Many small banks have gone out of business and we will feel more secure with a larger bank. Could we review that account balance sheets and all other documents?"

"Well Darling" Ben said with hesitation. He rephrased his remark, "Mrs. McCormick, I don't see that I have a hell of a lot of choices, do I?" Ben walked to the filing cabinets and removed two large file folders. He handed them to her and said, "I'll be outside, if you'll need me." He turned and walked out the door. He could not believe what was happening.

After about an hour, Mr. Clark, the attorney, came to the door and asked, "Mr. Lewis, could we see you, please?" Ben entered the office and took a chair. "Mr. Lewis, there seems to be a major problem. It appears that approximately forty thousand dollars worth of Federal Deposit Certificates are missing."

"They were replaced with promissory notes from this bank."

Mr. Stearns reiterated, "They are not worth the paper they are written on. How in the hell did you talk the Federal Reserve Bank into redeeming them?"

"Wasn't a problem, I had power of attorney for Marie during her absence. I presented them with the "Power of Attorney" and they had no choice but to redeem them.

"Didn't they require a Death Certificate?"

"Why should they? They didn't know she was dead."

"That was only good until her death. Those were the property of Mrs. McCormick and you were well aware of it."

"The Federal Reserve Bank didn't know that. Mrs. McCormick's name was not listed on the certificates."

"Mr. Lewis this is a serious problem," said Mr. Clark. "You are aware what the consequences could be, aren't you? You have stolen forty thousand dollars from your daughter."

"I have not stolen from her; I have borrowed from her account. I'm well aware of the consequences. I also have spent time in law school. There are only three choices for Mrs. McCormick. She can accept the promissory notes, file suit or press criminal charges. In the meantime, let's prepare the transfer of the account."

Sarah asked, "What about the furniture store and the ranch?"

"They belong to me. But for your information, the furniture store went bankrupt last year. The ranch has lost all cattle due to the draught and dust storms and the property has become a dust bowl. But Mrs. McCormick, that is no concern of yours at all."

The next morning Mr. Clark returned to the bank. Ben asked 'Where are Mrs. McCormick and Mr. Stearns?"

"They have already boarded the train for Baltimore, Mr. Lewis; Mrs. McCormick has decided not to press criminal charges at this time. We demand that the promissory notes be revised and the three year date be changed to two hundred and seventy days. That will allow you nine months to make restitution before we press charges."

"Why not allow me more time?"

"You said you had spent time in law school, surely you remember the advantages of filing within one year of the offence. Are you willing to revise the worthless notes?"

"You don't give me much of a choice. They will be paid on time or sooner." Ben changed the dates on the notes and then handed them to him and then said, "Mr. Clark would you be so kind as to get the hell out of my bank?" Clark nodded, turned and walked away.

Within the next six months, Ben was able to dispose of his holding in West Texas Telephone and Telegraph Company. Fortunately, this was one of the stocks that held seventy five percent of its original value during the crash. He was also able to sell one of his downtown office buildings to a Fort Worth Oil Company that was leasing the top two floors. He was then able to make payments on the promissory notes within four months.

After the banking incident, Ben and Sarah had very little communication. She sent him Christmas Cards, signed "Sarah and John" with no other correspondence. She did send an announcement of her grandson's birth. A card merely stated, "Your great grandson was born July 22, 1930. His name is "Benjamin John Bolton." She also included their address and phone number. There was no other correspondence.

By 1933, areas in the Southern Plains began to experience dust storms and eventually grew into a dust bowl. Wind velocities often ranged from thirty to sixty miles per hour, with Amarillo experiencing 192 dusters between January 1933 and February 1936. The worst dust storm in history occurred on a Sunday afternoon on

April 18, 1935. That date became known as "Black Sunday." Houses were literally filled with a fine dirt and silt driven by the fifty-mile-an-hour gale. Without question, this storm put the finishing touch of destruction to what faint hope the area had for any agriculture. Cattle, not knowing what to do, would run in circles eventually filling their lungs with silt and dust until they collapsed and died. Not only did livestock suffer but all wildlife was practically destroyed, with the exception of the rabbit. Without predators, the rabbit population exploded and for the next few years, they consumed all vegetation.

Most of the local farms and ranches were abandoned. Ben held deeds and mortgages on thousands of acres of land and was unable to receive payments. Buyers were non-existing. By 1936, he had disposed of all his downtown commercial buildings, including Marie's furniture store and his coal company at Brownwood. His holdings were reduced to approximately twenty per cent of what they were before the great depression began.

CHAPTER 21

Search For Grandson

Ben searches for his lost adopted grandson in 1931.

He had contacted his attorneys to find his lost grandson. He had never seen him and had the limited details of his birth. He was born in Jasper TX., Jasper County, on October 27, 1904. All that Ben knew of the boy was that he had a slight problem with his left hand. His attorneys told him that they had hired private investigators to search. Later they informed him that all adoption records were confidential and they were not able to access any information. "If they can't access the records, hire someone who can," Ben concluded.

His attorneys contacted him about three weeks later. "We may have some information that may be of interest. We have located a man that was born in Jasper Tx. on Oct 27, 1904 that had a slight deformity on his left hand. He was a ward of the state and was placed for adoption. After six months a family by the name Clafcliff adopted him. His name is Marty Clafcliff. After a few years they moved to Barksdale Texas where he spent his childhood. His father was in the windmill business.

"Where is he now?"

"The investigators have gone to Barksdale and should soon have more information."

"Let me know when they find out. And remember all of this is strictly confidential. Do you understand that?"

About two months later Ben received a Telegram stating, "We have located your subject. We will contact you soon."

The attorney came to visit Ben and told him, "Ben, are sure you want to pursue this project?"

"Hell yes. Why would I be paying you these big bucks, if I didn't want to pursue it?"

"Don't think you will like what we found."

"Just what in the hell did you find?"

"Your grandson is in prison in Hondo convicted of a felony of thief."

"What do you mean, 'My grandson?'" "I have not said he is my grandson and under no circumstances will you ever refer to him as my grandson. Do you understand what I'm telling you?"

"Yes sir."

"What the hell did he do?"

"He was adopted by a family by the name of Clafcliff. His father, Thalmage and his mother Barbara were very good providers. Thalmage was in the windmill business and Marty began working with him at a young age. His dad was injured in a fall from a windmill tower. He was no longer able to drive and climb the towers. Marty had to do the duties his father was no longer able to do, supporting the family. He was selling and installing windmills in south Texas and was very busy, having very little opportunity for schooling. He dropped out of school after completing the eighth grade. He had met another young man, John Morris, also in the windmill business in Kingsville, Texas. They had met several times at a local bar, which had become a frequent pastime for Marty. They became very good friends and came up with a scheme to steal the motors from windmills of that area and Marty would take his pilferage to Ozona and they would exchange the stolen goods. There were no serial numbers involved and the profit margin was quite large. They had made a very lucrative business before the scheme was uncovered. Marty was sentenced to fifteen years in prison which he is now severing in the Department of Correction in Hondo Texas. He has served two years.

"What county was he tried in and do you know what court?"

"He was tried in Crockett County, fourth criminal court, Judge Harper presiding. Would you like for me can get a copy of the transcript?"

"No need, I have enough information. Oh by the way, do you know his T.D.C. number?"

"It is TDC8513903, anything else, sir?"

"No, was there anything about a bad left hand?"

"Yes, he has a slight problem with his left hand, but he can cope with that and there is no handicap movement whatsoever. He can do anything anyone else can do."

"Are you sure he was born in Jasper Texas on October 27, 1904?"

"There is no doubt about it."

"Thank you. I will no longer need your services. Please submit a bill for your services to my secretary and she will pay you in full. There is one other thing, as I have said before; I do not know you and you do not know me. All of this is strictly confidential. Do you understand what I'm telling you?'"

"Yes sir. Thank you and I will be available if you need me again," the investigator said as he walked away.

CHAPTER 22

Governor Visit

"Mary, send a telegram to Governor Dan Moody and tell him I want to meet with him as soon as possible. If he does not respond within two days, let me know."

Ben received a telegram two days later from the governor stating, "I can meet with you on Friday, February 10, 1931 at two o'clock. If this is not convenient for you please notify me immediately."

"Mary send a telegram to Governor Moody and tell him I will be there Friday at two o'clock. Make travel arrangements accordingly."

Friday afternoon Ben was escorted into the governor's office. "Hey, come on in Ben, how have you been?" They shook hands and each took a chair.

"Not too bad, I have been very busy. This economy is hard on the banking business. How is Mildred doing?"

"She is doing fine. She stays busy taking care of the two boys. How have you been doing after Marie's death?"

"As well as could be expected, governor. If I could, I would like to get to business and not take a lot of your time."

"Sure, Ben, but I always have time for you. What can I do for you?"

"There is a young man in prison at Hondo, Cell Block K. His name is Marty Calfcliff. His number is TDC8511903. He has served two years on a fifteen year sentence for theft. I want him pardoned immediately."

"There is no way I can do that. I have never pardoned anyone and I don't intend to for you or anyone else. In a case of pardon, the newspapers will have a hay day with it. They will try to come up with some kind of scandal. Why would you ask for a pardon?"

"I want this man's slate cleared. You know damn well that Marie and I have contributed many times to your political career and I have never asked you for a damn thing in return. I hate to bring it up, but you remember the highway construction project that went sour for you. I was C.E.O. of Texas Telephone and Telegraph at that time. You remember the construction company destroying twelve miles of our telephone equipment? As best I remember, I think your brother-in-law owned the company. I did not pursue damages, at your request, because you had enough problems at that time. I told you then that I may ask you to return the favor someday."

"Who is this guy? Is he a relative of yours?"

"I want him out of there and I do not want my name mentioned in any way. As a personal friend, could you take care of it and keep my involvement strictly confidential?"

"Ben, I will not pardon him. I have a lot of influence with the parole board and I can be of help in that capacity, but the slate won't be clean. They can be pretty hard nosed about paroling. It may go easy unless he is a troublemaker. If that is the case, they will make him serve at least half his sentence. Do you know anything about his record?"

"The only thing I know is he is in prison and I want him out."

"Ben, this is very unusual. What is your interest in this case? You know the board is going to ask me about my involvement. I need to tell them something or I will be talking to deaf ears. I don't want to have to demand a release, although I could."

"I'm sure you can come up with something, you never seemed to have a problem with it in the past. As I said, I do not want my name mentioned in any way. I have never met him and I know only one thing about him, he was dealt a great injustice at a young age. I would like to see him get some kind of a break. I hired a private investigator to obtain the information I needed. Once the investigation was completed, I told them to destroy all records of my involvement. I can get you a court transcript of his trial, that's all."

"Ben, we have been friends for many years. I appreciate all you and Marie have done for me in the past. I will see what I can do. I will be in touch."

They stood and shook hands. Ben turned to walk away and said "Give my best to Mildred and the boys."

CHAPTER 23

Ranch Foreclosure

On April 22 1931, Ben was to attend court in Stephens County Texas on a foreclosure of a 6,000 acre ranch near Breckenridge, Texas. He contacted the Rancher, Fred William Bronson, and made an appointment to meet the day before the court proceedings. He arrived at the ranch and was welcomed by Mr. Bronson.

"Fred we have been doing business for over twenty years. I am very sorry that things have come to this. I have been under tremendous pressure since the bank crash and I have no other choice but to proceed with the process. I have a buyer for the property, but I will suffer a great loss. My biggest concern is your future, however. What will you do?"

"Ben you are a very good friend and I know that if there was another way out, you would find a way to pursue it. Ben, I know ranching. This is all I have ever done. My father settled here in 1859. At that time Breckenridge was called Picketville and was in Buchanan, now Stephens County. When he was building the first cabin, he found a Spanish spur that was broken. That's where he got the name of the ranch. The spur still hangs over the fire place. I'm 76 years old and I really don't know what I will do without this ranch. I had a good herd but the drought almost broke me, as it wiped out all the other ranchers. You couldn't give a cow away back then. My wife died four years ago. I know that you know what that is like having been through the same lost. We had two sons Joe, the older, was killed at Ft. Worth in a drunken bar-room fight in 1896, he was too full of piss-n- vinegar. Denton, the younger, drowned in 1908, trying to cross Hubbard Creek during a flash flood. That was a foolish thing he did. He was riding a colt that was barely broken. It panicked crossing the creek and the water was too swift. If he had waited a few hours the water would have gone down. That almost killed me and his mother. You know Ben, I have no family to leave the ranch to, but I just hate to lose it.

"Fred, My dad was a wealthy man at one time. He was a cotton broker, involved in building a railroad and owned a fifteen hundred acre cotton plantation in Columbia County Arkansas. He had mortgaged the plantation to support his railroad. The Civil War broke him. He had thirty-one slaves. They were freed. Most went back to Mississippi where they came from and the rest just spread throughout the country. A few hung around the plantation and helped him plant a few crops. He had big dreams of my brother becoming a lawyer but he was killed in October of 1862 fighting for the Confederacy. My dad lost the plantation, but was able to hold the house and two hundred acres of land. When the bankers foreclosed on him, I hated them for it and I'll be damned if I didn't become one. After the war, he became quite wealthy in the cotton business. He had it set up for me to go to Law School. I went to Baltimore and got a Law Degree and a wife. I desperately need to recover some of the capitol that I have lost over the past years." After a moment of silence, Ben asked, "Fred, I hope we are able come up with a solution to this problem. I'm just curious, what was your plan for the ranch at your time of death?"

"I'm the only one left. I have a niece and nephew that live somewhere in Washington State. I haven't seen or heard from them in almost thirty years. If they knew they were in line for my estate, whatever is left, they might be paying me a visit, reckon?" he said with a laugh. What in the hell do you have in mind, Ben?"

"According to the financial statements you have submitted, all your assets, ranch, cattle, home and equipment are worth approximately $203,000. You owe the bank $169,482. "

"The net worth sounds mighty low to me."

"You've got to remember Fred, these are banker's figures," he said with a smile. I know a potential buyer, who said he may be willing to pay you $175,000. That won't leave you a hell of lot of money after paying the bank."

"Ben, a man my age living in town, won't need a hell of a lot of money, but it is something I'm not looking forward to. I know I'm in a lot of trouble. I have had to sell too many cattle to try to meet obligations. I don't have the capital to stock the ranch to its full potential. It seems that I dig a deeper hole each year. Maybe you can find a buyer that is willing to pay a little more?"

"Hell, Fred, you are not the only one who is in trouble. People with money now are getting bargains and the landowners are the ones that are suffering. Fred, I am willing to extend the financing. You will not have to make payments on principle or interest. You will have to agree to my accountants to auditing all transactions and you can operate as you always have. This agreement will be in effect as long as you live, but there are other stipulations."

"What other stipulations?"

"Fred, I have had a group of attorneys helping me with this deal. I have ways of covering your obligations at the bank, although, I will have to dispose of other properties, at a loss, I might add. I can use those funds to cover this deal, if you agree. This deal must be strictly confidential for personal reasons. This is not a money-laundering operation, but the least said, the fewer questions will be asked."

"I assure you, if you can save my ass, I'll never say a word to anyone. That is unless I'm in a court of law and then I won't lie."

"I wouldn't expect you to. If there are any questions asked, that will be after you are dead and gone. At my age, that will be several years after I'm gone. Are you interested in hearing more?"

"Why hell yes, I want to hear more."

"Fred, if you don't agree, you will lose everything and I truly don't want that to happen. There are two other requirements. First, there is a young man in prison in Hondo that will be free soon and he will be looking for a job. He will be your ranch foreman and his pay will equal to what your interest payments have been in the past. The lien will be removed from the ranch in a very discreet way, if you are willing to will it to him upon your death. Are you interested?"

"Why, hell yes I'm interested. My prayers have been answered. Who is this new ranch foreman I'm hiring?"

"All I know is that his name is Marty Calfcliff. To be honest with you, I have never seen him or talked to him and that is the way I want it to be. You must never disclose this arrangement to him and never mention my name. If you are in agreement, I will notify the court that an agreement has been made and my attorneys will stop the foreclosure proceedings. They will contact you later today."

"That's a deal, bring them on." They shook hands and Ben turned and started to walk away.

He stopped and said, "There is one other thing. I had figured the property was worth about $200,000 and you owe me about $170,000. That's a difference of about $30,000. A man will be calling on you with a $30,000 check. Write him a bill of sale for that amount of cattle."

"Ben, I don't have $30,000 worth of livestock on this ranch."

"You and I know that but no one else does. He doesn't want your stock. All he will want is a bill of sale where he bought them. Take the money and go to a cattle sale and buy yourself and Marty some good stock. We need to change this ranch into a money maker."

They shook hands and as Ben was walking away, "Ben, one other thing, what name do I put on this, bogus Bill of Sale?

Ben replied as he continued to walk away, "Marie Lewis Cattle Company."

Fred was thinking to himself, "Who in the hell is this Marty Calfcliff?"

CHAPTER 24

Texas Department Of Correction, Hondo Texas

On Tuesday May 5, 1931, Cell Block K had finished their breakfast when Captain McDonald ordered them to meet at the north end of the exercise yard. Cell block K contained twenty inmates of a non-violent nature. Most were serving sentences for petty felony offences. Marty became popular and became "Cell block K's" mediator. He always had a smile on his face and he was able to find humor with almost all situations. His laughter and joke telling was very uplifting to the convicts. Even the guards became friendlier and more cordial toward him and cell block K. On occasions the guards were reprimanded for being too easy on the "Boys of K".

"Hey Captain, we going on a picnic today?" Marty yelled.

"Yep, you're going to be doing some picking and nicking."

"Can we bring our baseball equipment with us and have a ball game?'

"You bring your balls and a pair of gloves but you want need a bat because you are going to be holding a hoe handle. We are going to hoe field number 17." Laughter broke out throughout the cafeteria.

Marty said holding up his left hand, "Captain, I got a bad hand, it don't fit a hoe handle."

"It'll fit after I lay a whip across your ass."

"I got a damn good idea. If you'll let me out of here for a few days, I'll steal us some sheep and in a few days they'll pick field 17 as slick as a baby's ass while we're playing baseball."

"Marty, this ain't a damn picnic, it's a prison. Stealing is what got you here in the first place. If I were you, I'd remove the word "stealing" from your vocabulary."

"Ye right, captain, I'll borrow them and then take them back when the game is over."

"I've heard enough shit out of you. Keep your damn mouth shut and don't say another word, "McDonald said in a stern voice, again the cafeteria was filled with laughter.

Marty had seen that he was pressing his luck enough for the time being. The whistle blew and they made their way for the exercise yard. They assembled in a line and the guards handcuffed each of them which were a requirement any time they left the compound. They were loaded in a bus type vehicle and were transported to field 17. McDonald and another guard were waiting on horseback. The cuffs were removed and they went single file to retrieve their large hoe. They were placed in a straight line and McDonald yelled "There will be no talking and I want each hoe hitting the ground at the same time. Keep a straight line or you'll get the whip across your ass. Do I make myself clear?"

Marty said, "Yes sir, I still think the sheep is a better idea."

"Marty, damn your sole, you're going to force me to put the whip to your ass," he said with a big smile on his face. "I don't want to hear another word from you. Do you understand?"

"Not another word, Captain."

McDonald blew his whistle and yelled "Go." They began chopping the grass in silence. The only sound was the hoes hitting the ground and rocks. Suddenly there was a "Baah-Baah" sheep blatting sound which came from the far end of the line. McDonald rode toward the sound trying to conceal the smile on his face.

"Which one of you smart asses are blatting like a sheep?"

"We didn't hear anything."

"If I hear that again, I'll," but before he finished the sentence another "Baha-Baha" came from the other end of the line. He realized that he had better get used to the blatting, which he was seeing some humor in himself. The other guard, who was a new recruit, was looking forward to using his whip.

McDonald yelled, "Halt". The line stopped hoeing and they stood at attention. He rode to Marty and said, "I know you are behind all this "sheep blatting" bull shit and the new guard is going to whack someone. You had better advice the men to stop or someone is going to get a whelp on their back."

"Captain, you ain't heard a "peep" from me. If they "blate" like a sheep and he wants to pop their ass, it ain't no skin off my back."

McDonald ordered them to work and a few seconds later someone said "Peep". He just shook his head and said with a big smile, "Marty, you are making my job mighty tough. You see the new guard? I'm not sure he is not spying for the warden. The warden has threatened to move me to another compound if I cannot control you boys. Pass the word to the boys not to have any more fun today." A few minutes later the only sounds were the hoes chopping the grass.

On the third day, after the lunch truck had arrived and lunches passed out, the end mates gathered under a tree and ate lunch. One guard would have lunch while the other circled the end mates on horseback. As McDonald came near, Marty yelled, "Hey Captian, are you a Catholic?"

"It is none of your damn business what I am."

"I was just wondering how they made that holly water."

"The priest blesses it, you dumb ass."

"Oh, that's how they do it. I though they just boiled the hell out it."

McDonald smiled and said, "I'm going to eat. Don't be joking with the new guard or we both may regret it."

As they were returning to work, another prison vehicle came driving into the field. McDonald went to meet the prison official. They talked for a few minutes and then McDonald came to Marty with a pair of cuffs and told him to put his hands behind his back; he cuffed him and led him to the waiting vehicle. McDonald whispered, "I hope your joking is not the reason for transferring you to another unit."

Someone yelled, "Where ye goin, Marty?"

"Going to get us a flock of sheep," he said with a big smile on his face.

The end mates began to quiz McDonald as what was going on. "I don't know any more than you do and it ain't any of your damn business. Now get your asses to work." The rest of the day the end mates worked in silence without blatting and peeping.

Marty was taken to his cell and told to put on clean coveralls and change shoes. The guard then said, "I'll be back in a few minutes." The guard returned and he was ushered to the main office. The handcuffs were removed and he was then told to sit outside a door until he was called. A few minutes later he was called into a conference room with five people sitting at a table. There were nameplates in front of each stating their names. Before sitting in his designated chair, Marty walked to Mr. Morris and extended his hand. "Mr. Morris, it's a pleasure to meet you. Without saying anything, Mr. Morris shook his hand. "That's a nice suit you're wearing."

Mr. Morris was somewhat forced to respond. "Thank you, Mr. Clafcliff." Before he was able to tell him to have a seat, Marty had extended his hand to Mr. Watson.

"You all can call me "Marty", if you like." He extended his hand to Mr. Watson and said, "Mr. Watson, thanks for seeing me, it's nice to meet you. I really like that shirt. Did you pick it out or is your wife responsible? He asked with a big smile on his face.

Watson smiled and replied, "My wife."

Next Marty offered his hand to Mrs. Holland. She was an elderly lady, the mat idée type, with her glasses resting on the end of her noise, her hair in a layered bund on top of her head. "Mrs. Holland, nice hairdo. You must have stopped at the hair shop on your way in this afternoon. It is very becoming and I don't see a hair out of place.

She chuckled and said, "I can assure you Marty, It's usually a mess".

Before Marty could complement the other two members, Mr. Morris said, "Mr. Calfcliff, please have a seat." Marty shook hands with the other members without saying anything else.

The chairman said, "Mr. Calfcliff, we have received a request to review your case. This an unusual case, in that we do not consider probation when someone has served only two years of a fifteen year sentence. We understand that you were stealing windmills. Is that correct?"

"Yes sir, but only the motors and sometimes the blades, if I didn't damage them to badly when I dropped them to the ground."

"We understand that it would be hard to steal a whole windmill, wouldn't it? You want to tell us about it?"

"Yes sir. I sold and serviced windmills in several counties in south Texas. I had one competitor in the area and he and I didn't get along to well. I would travel the country and give free inspections for my customers. I would then report to the customer, the mill number, the condition and the recommended repair or replacement, if I felt any were needed. I took good care of my customers and they took good care of me. One day the sheriff paid me a visit and informed me that some motors had been stolen and my truck had been seen on the ranch. I was not aware of any equipment theft and I never went on any ranch except those of my customers. My customers had not suffered any lost. About two weeks later the sheriff came to see me again and questioned me about another theft. I was innocent. Then I heard of a man in San Angelo who dealt in used windmill equipment. I paid him a visit and asked if he knew my competitor. They did business regularly. I felt like I was being set up by my competitor. I decided to fight fire with fire. I then began to steal from his customers. I would re-condition and re-paint them and then sell them to my customers or to another dealer at Kingsville. After several months I was busted."

"Have you ever been in jail before this?"

"Only one time, I was arrested for an assault."

"Tell us about it."

"It was a barroom fight. I had never fought before, that's a good way to get hurt. Several of us had a little too much to drink. We were laughing and having a good time when some cowboy thought we were laughing too much. I made some funny remark, which was a mistake, and everyone laughed except him. He came for me. I was scared because I don't like to fight. I opened my knife and we wrestled around for a while. I didn't stab him but I did slice him in a couple of places. They arrested us both and put us in jail. The next morning I went before the judge and he asked how I pleaded. I told him "Self Defense due to Intoxication Insanity." The judge found that quite funny and said he had never had anyone plea that before. He asked if I was sure it was self-defense. I told him, "It was self-defense, but if I hadn't been suffering from Intoxication insanity, I would have run. That is the only fight I was ever in. He charged me with disturbing the peace and he fined me $200 and let me go. I don't know what he did to the other guy."

The board members were smiling as Marty told of the incidence. The chairman said with a big smile, "Mr. Calfcliff that will be all." A guard came and escorted him from the room and returned him to his cell. About 3: o'clock the guard came and got him and said, "The warden wants to see you."

As they were walking down the hall, one of the end mates asked "What's this all about, Marty?"

"I think the warden is going to send me to buy us some sheep," he said a big smile on his face.

He was escorted to the warden's office. The warden was sitting behind a large desk with a folder placed on it. He looked up at Marty and said, "You god damn punk, sat down and don't say a damn word unless I asks you too." He stood, placed his hands on the desk and leaned forward until his face was within inches from Marty's face. "You are a god damn thief; the world would be a better place if you rotted in this hell hole." He then returned to his chair. "I run this place and I'm not in favor of ever letting any of you rotten bastards out, but Unfortunanly, sometimes I'm forced to offer probation. I'm sure you heard me say "offer". By no means do you have to accept and I hope you reject the offer because I ain't through with you yet. If you accept, you'll probably be back in a few months and you think you have had it tough now, you ain't seen anything yet. I'll promise you one thing, if you come back the second time; I'll be so damn hard on you that I'll guarantee you'll not come back the third. The conditions of this probation are very unusual but I'm not the one to determine them. They are: You will be placed under the supervision of a rancher in northwest Texas by the name of Fred Bronson. I have no idea who in the hell he is. I just hope he is one mean son of a bitch. You will remain under his supervision for the duration of your sentence. You will be assigned a probation officer in that county and you are to report to him as directed. Any violations or if you have a warrant of any kind, there will be no hearing and your stinking ass will be back in my control. "Do you understand?

"Yes sir."

"Do you accept the terms?"

"Yes sir and I ---"

Before he could finish the statement, the warden stopped him and said, "I told you not to say a damn word unless I asked for it. All I wanted hear was a yes or no. I want your sorry stinky ass out of my office, right now." He handed the folder to Marty and finished by saying, "Give this to the guard."

He was escorted to his cell to gather his personal belongings. The guard gave him a few minutes and told him he would return later.

A few minutes' later two guards returned and put handcuffs on him and told him to follow. "There is someone waiting for you at the front gate". As they walked down the hall, end mates yelled, "Marty what are they going to do to you?

He smiled and said, "Set me free. If I get a chance, I'll send you guys some sheep for Christmas".

On May 5, 1931, at four o'clock he was escorted to the front gate and the cuffs were removed. One of the guards opened the folder and removed an envelope and handed it to him. "You earned a little traveling money, bet you thought you were working for nothing." Each guard shook hands with him and wished him luck. They opened the front gate and as he stepped out onto the sidewalk, an elderly man was standing by a one ton truck. On the door was written "Broken Spur Ranch, Breckenridge, Texas. The man asked, "are you Marty Calfcliff?'

"Yes I am, A Free Marty Calfcliff, I might add," with a big smile on his face.

The man extended his hand and said, "I'm Fred Bronson, are you ready to do a little ranching."

"You bet, let's get the hell away from this place," Marty said as they were getting into the truck.

When leaving, Fred turned east on Highway 90 and said, "we'll stay in Austin tonight. In the morning we will go to Brownwood and pick up your new truck. You do have a driver licenses, don't you?"

Smiling Marty said, "As a matter of fact, I don't. I think they have expired."

Fred said, "Don't guess you have been doing a lot of driving lately. You do know how to drive, don't you?"

"Sure but what do you mean, pick up my truck?"

"If you are going to run my ranch, you'll need a good truck."

Marty sat without saying anything for a long time. His expression had changed from a big smile to a look of puzzlement. Finally he asked "Would you please tell me what the hell is taking place? Why would I be receiving such a good fortune? Just who in the hell are you?"

Fred looked at him, smiled and said, "Don't ask too many questions or I'll turn around and take you back to Hondo." Marty sat in disbelief.

They arrived in Austin, checked into a motel and went next door to a restaurant for dinner. They ordered their food and Fred said, "I think this occasion calls for a drink. What do you think?

"That sounds good to me. I never was much of a drinker and it's been over two years since I've had one. I may get a little tipsy."

Fred said, "Hell, let's have enough to make us tipsy so we can sleep tonight. Do you know anything about ranching?"

"A little but one thing for sure, I'll keep your wind mills in good shape," he said with a smile.

"After we get your truck, you will follow me to a ranch outside of town. I have bought a few head of cattle and I dropped the trailer off there on the way to get you. We'll be late getting home tomorrow night. After we get them home and you get settled in, you can take a few days to visit your friends and relatives. First thing we must do is get you your driver license."

After the meal was complete, the waitress laid the food ticket on the table. Marty removed the envelope from his pocket to count his money the guard had given him. "Put that back in your pocket. You are an employee of the Broken Spur and along with that comes an expense account."

"Mr. Bronson, you need to help me with something. You said that you bought cattle in Brownwood and dropped the trailer off there. You then bought a truck for me. You were at Hondo to pick me up at four o'clock. My hearing wasn't until around one thirty this afternoon. I don't know what time they decided to turn me loose but there is no way in hell you would've had time to drive from Brownwood and pick me up at four o'clock unless you knew before hand."

"You are pretty clever. I knew last week that you would walk out around four o'clock today. You might say that I know people in high places. But don't ask me any questions, just be thankful the way things are."

"Are you telling me that the board hearing was a bunch of bull shit?"

"That was just a formality to keep the records straight"

"I wish I had known and then I wouldn't have lied. I would have told Mr. Morris that his suit looked like something a person would buy at the Salvation Army. I would have told Mr. Watson that a damn clown wouldn't be caught dead in the shirt he was wearing and I would have told Mrs. Holland that her hair-do looked like a cow had shit on top of her head." They both went into a laughing frenzy.

The next morning after they had breakfast, Marty asked, "Mr. Bronson is there some way I can notify my parents that I'm free." He removed the envelope and counted his money, he had $129.00. "I have enough money. My folks don't have a phone but a neighbor does. They will give them the message."

"Sure, we will find the phone office." A few minutes later the call was made.

On their way to Brownwood, Bronson asked, "Did you sleep good last night?"

"To be honest, I don't think I slept a wink. I was too excited. I can't figure out what is happening to me. I keep wondering who you are. It seems like a dream."

"It ain't a dream, get use to it."

The two and half hour drive to Brownwood seemed quite short. Marty entertained Fred with constant joke telling. They went to the Chevrolet House and got the truck, then drove to the ranch and loaded the cattle. They arrived at the Broken Spur Ranch near one the next morning. Jake and Bruce, the two ranch hands met them and the cattle were unloaded. "Jake, show Marty to the bunk house. I'll see you'll all in the morning"

During the next few days, Marty had moved into his new living quarters, which was a two bedroom house adjacent to the main house. He had received his driving license and had the "ranch logo" painted on the doors of his new truck.

Fred gave Marty $100 and told him to take a few days off and go visit friends and relatives. "Get rid of those prison issued brogan boots and get you some cowboy boots. On your way back go to the Farm Store in Abilene and get six rolls of barb wire. We need to build a fence. Be back in a week or ten days."

Marty got into the truck and said with a big smile on his face, "I have boots at Mom's house, if she hadn't thrown them away. See you in a few days."

"One other thing, don't drive that truck if you have been drinking."

"Don't worry, that will never be a problem," he said. He then got out of the truck and walked to Fred with a serious look on his face. "Mr. Bronson, there is something that I need to talk to you about."

"Sure, what's on your mind?"

"There is a girl in Campwood and her name is Susan McWilliams. She has been my sweetheart since high school. I had asked her to marry me when I got out of prison and believe it or not, she said she would be happy too. Do you have any objections if I bring a wife back with me?"

"Of course not, if you are sure that's what you want," he said with a big smile on his face. "Maybe that's what this ranch needs, is woman's touch. If you do marry her, I'll treat her like a daughter and you like a son in law, which means, if you mistreat her, you'll have hell to pay with me."

Marty and Susan were married May 29, 1931. When they returned to the ranch, Marty yelled to Fred, "I got you some barb-wire and me a wife."

CHAPTER 25

Ben And Marty Meet

In 1933, the phone rang at the Lewis residence and was answered by a man with a Spanish accent, "Hello, this is the Lewis Residence."

"Is Ben in?"

"No sir. Mr. Ben doesn't live here much of the time. He lives at the Garden Place."

"This is Fred Branson. What's the Garden Place?'

"It's an assisted-living home. Mr. Ben's health is not very good and he lives there for them to care of him. He got to where he didn't like my cooking" the man said with a chuckle. "I guess he would rather have women take care of him."

"I am in town and I wanted him to have dinner with me tonight. Do you think he would be able to meet? Do you have a phone number for him?"

"Yes I do. On Fridays I take him to dinner and we usually come here to spend the night and then I take him back the next morning. I'll pick him and Mr. Railroad up around five o'clock and we go to

The Cattlemen's for dinner. I'm sure Mr. Lewis would be thrilled if you met us there. We usually get there about five-thirty."

"I'll be there around five-thirty. Will that be o. k.?"

"Sure see you then."

Fred and Marty arrived before the others. Fred asked Marty to go inside and reserve a table for them. Marty went inside as they drove into the parking lot. Felix stopped at the door and Fred met them and opened the door for Ben. He helped Ben from the car and they shook hands, both laughing from the excitement of seeing each other. "How in the world have you been doing?"

"Not too bad for an old man, what about you?"

"Great," Fred replied.

"Do you remember Railroad Dockery?'

"Sure, we met at Sarah's wedding. That was a long time ago."

They shook hands and Railroad said, "That was sure enough a long time ago. I don't think Mrs. Marie was too happy with me back then. It took her a while, but she finally got use to having me around."

Felix had parked the car and had joined the company at the door. "Ben, I forgot to mention it, but my ranch foreman has gone inside to get us a table. Hope you don't mind."

Ben looked at him with a surprised look on his face and said, "Fred, I would have been very disappointed if he hadn't come."

As they entered the door, Marty came to meet them. Ben stood speechless as Marty offered his hand. Ben could hardly keep from staring at him. He was six feet tall, light brown hair, blue eyes, a round face and was wearing a big smile. He could see features of both Sarah and Charlene in him. There was no doubt in Ben's mind that he was his lost grandson. They shook hands and went to the table.

Marty said, "I think this calls for a drink, what you all think?"

Fred and Ben agreed. Felix ordered ice tea and Railroad ordered a beer. "I can't drink the hard stuff," Railroad said laughing, "My wife tells me when I've had a few drinks, I talk with my African dialect and white people can't understand half of what I say."

"I thought Mrs. Effie put a stop to that nigger talk," Ben said laughing.

Railroad continued, recounting, "The first day of school when it was time for Ben's dad to pick us up, I said "Bout time fur yo papie to come and git us." Mrs. Effie made repeat ten times 'It is about time for your father to come get us.' I remember Master John laughing; he thought that was so funny. She swatted me many times for not speaking properly." They all had a good laugh. He continued, "My wife, Margie is educated and has spent over twenty five years trying to make me talk like a white man. If I were to come home with too many drinks under my belt and talking like a nigger, she would probably shoot me. I thank the lord for her and Mrs. Effie each day."

"Marty asked "Do you have children?"

"Yes we do, we have two sons and one daughter. The oldest boy, guess what his name is? Benjamin Lewis Dockery, named after my best friend." Railroad announced as he pointed to Ben. "The other two are named Roosevelt and Dora. They were named after the servants of the Lambertine Plantation. Ben lives in St. Louis, he is a painter. Roosevelt and Dora live here in Amarillo."

"Railroad is one of the best artists in the state of Texas, his son inherited his talent," Ben added.

Marty said, "Be thankful Railroad. If god gave me a talent, I ain't found it yet."

"Bull shitting is your talent," Fred remarked, laughing

"Mr. Lewis, I take it that you are retired," Marty asked of Ben. "What business were you in?"

"I have been in banking and real estate, mostly banking, but I have become too damn old for that now. I try to stay involved a little, but it's not as much fun as it used to be. The depression almost took care of the bank and the dust bowl took care of the real estate." Ben then asks, "How are things going at the Broken Spur?" The conversation then moved from banking to the ranching business.

The waitress came for a repeat drink order and asked Marty "You from around here? I ain't seen you in here before."

"No, I'm from a small place you never heard of, Cale, Texas. There ain't nothing there but a crossroad, two stores, two whores and a cotton gin."

She laughed and said "I bet you know both of them."

Marty was continuously telling funny stories and they all laughed at his humor and his way of entertaining.

During dinner, Ben thought of many questions that he would like to ask Marty but avoided most of them. "Marty, how old are you?"

"I am twenty nine; I was born October 27, 1904 in east Texas."

"How is Fred to work for? I always thought he would be hell to get along with. Maybe he has mellowed in his old age," Ben said with a big smile.

"He is a lot better than my last employer, although he always gives me the tougher jobs. I hold the calves while he castrates them. I stretch the wire and he drives the staples. I have to shovel the shit, even with a bad hand," he said with a chuckle as he showed his left hand. Nothing more was mentioned of his last employer.

After the meal and conversation had dulled, Fred suggested that they call it a night. Ben agreed though he was not ready for the night to end. He said, "I can't remember when I have laughed so much. I have plenty of room at my place. Why don't you and Marty spend the night with me?"

"We would like too, but I need to get Marty back to the ranch and put his ass to work," Fred said as he winked at Ben. Ben returned with a big smile and a nod of thanks. "I promise we will come back again, soon."

When they returned to The Garden Place, Felix got out of the car and helped Ben to his feet. As they were walking to the door Ben said, "Felix, you go ahead and go, Railroad can help me in." They bid Felix good night as he drove away.

"You got time to visit for a while?" Ben asked.

"Sure Ben, I've always got time for you."

"I've a secret that has been bothering me for many years. I realize my health won't last much longer and I know I should take it to the grave with me, but I want to share it with you. The funny man who entertained us at dinner tonight is my grandson." The two men then sat silently for a moment. Railroad said nothing but was visibly shocked by the news. "You know how Marie was, didn't give a damn for anybody but herself. She was really pissed off when she got pregnant with Sarah. I was excited myself. Marie always had a governess take care of her and then shipped her off to Baltimore when she was twelve years old. I should have stood up to her then, but you could not argue with her. Sarah became pregnant at age seventeen. Marie forced her to put the kid up for adoption. I raised all kind of hell with Marie, but I finally let her have her way, as usual. Sarah and I never saw the child, but Marie did. She told me the adoption was the best solution because he had a deformed hand. Two fingers were not fully developed on his left hand and no telling what other problems he may have. Did you notice his small fingers on the left hand?"

"Yes, I noticed. Didn't seem to bother him any. I enjoyed being with him, he is a funny man."

"He is Fred's ranch foreman and I didn't know they were coming tonight, but I'm sure glad they did. I have often wondered what he was like. He and I could have really enjoyed each other if only I had had the guts to stand up to Marie. He favors Sarah a lot."

"Does Mr. Bronson know who he is?"

"No, Railroad. You and I are the only people who know. I just didn't want to take the secret to my grave. I hope you don't mind me telling you."

"Not at all. After all, we are brothers ain't we?"

"I'll tell you another secret if you promise not to laugh."

With a smile Railroad responded, "I promise. What's that?"

"At dad's funeral, I became so attracted to Mississippi that I could not get my mind off her. We weren't but seventeen at the time. She was the most beautiful woman I had ever seen."

Railroad smiled and said, "Ben, I knew your feelings for her. As careful as you were choosing your words when you wrote her letters, I could tell when I read them to her."

"When I was going to school at Magnolia, I went to see her, but she and Bessie had gone to the Mississippi Delta area in eastern Arkansas. That broke my heart. They took the last name of "Lewis", the same as my family. I didn't care if she was considered to be black. I would have married her in a New York minute. We could have been happy. There was no way to make Marie happy. If I had everything to do over, I would never marry a wealthy woman. Someday, white and black will marry and people won't think a thing about it. It may be another one hundred years before that happens."

"Your right, things will be different in a few years. Mississippi made some man a good wife. I just hope she didn't spend her entire life in a cotton field."

"Thanks for letting me share my thoughts. It's getting late. I better go in before they lock me out."

They walked to the door. Railroad held it open and as Ben entered. Railroad said, "Good night, brother."

CHAPTER 26

The Death Of Ben

On May 1, 1936, Railroad had reported to his office when the phone rang. Ruth, his secretary called him to the phone. "Railroad, this is Mary, I'm at General Hospital. They have brought Ben here and it appears that he is suffering from cardiac arrest. I thought I should call and let you know what has happened."

"Thanks, Mary. I'll be right there"

When he arrived at the hospital, Felix and Mary were standing in the hallway. The door opened and a doctor came to them. "We did everything possible to save him but, his heart had suffered too much damage. I'm truly sorry. Is there anything I can do to help you?"

Mary was first to replied, "No, thanks Doctor. We can handle things," the doctor turned and walked away. Mary then looked at Railroad and asked if he would call Sarah, as she handed him a paper with her phone number.

"Sure Mary, anything I can do, just let me know," he said with a trembling voice. "But first, I need to be alone for a while."

"Take your time Railroad. I want to talk to you before you call her. I will be in the main lobby near the front door."

After a few minutes he met Mary in the lobby. "Ben had made all arrangements for the service. He asked if you would read the obituary."

"If he wanted me to, I will do my best. I'm not accustomed to speaking before a group and I'm afraid I may become emotional."

"You will do fine. I have everything written and all you will need to do is read what I give you."

Railroad found a public phone and dialed Sarah's number. She recognized his voice immediately, "Railroad, Dad has died, hasn't he?"

"Yes ma'am. He died a few minutes ago from a heart attack. If there is anything I can do for you, I'll be more than happy. Let me give you my phone number and if you think of anything, just let me know."

"I'll come as quickly as possible to make arrangements."

"That will not be necessary, Sarah. He had already made all arrangements for the service. He must have known he didn't have a lot of time. The date of the service will depend on you and your family, but all else is pretty well taken care of."

"I'll call John and Charlene and we will decide when we can get there. I'll call you later today."

"Alright. I'm really sorry Mrs. Sarah, just let me know."

Sarah called later that evening and informed Railroad of their arrival on Thursday. She asked, if the service could be on Saturday in case of traveling problems. Mary contacted the funeral home to see if they could accommodate the Saturday afternoon request. She then called the newspaper and furnished the obituary with service details. She then called a number of Ben's friends to inform them of his passing.

Sarah and John arrived at the train depot Thursday afternoon. They took a taxi to the home. When they arrived there, they saw signs attached to the doors. "NO TRASPASSING Orders of Potter County Sherriff's Department."

They then went to Felix's living quarters and asked for a key to the residence. He informed them that he had no keys, the sheriff had taken them.

"Why in the hell would they do that?" she asked.

"I don't know, they came with the signs and told me to give them all the keys."

Sarah turned to John and said, "Let's go visit the sheriff". She then turned to Felix and asked, "Can we use the car?"

"Sure," he replied as he handed them the keys.

On their way downtown, Sarah asked, "John, do you think this is unusual for them to lock the house?"

"It's to your advantage, Sarah. They may have locked it to keep Felix and his friends from carting away your valuables."

When they arrived at the sheriff's office she said, "I'm Sarah McCormick, Ben Lewis's daughter and I am here to get the keys to my house."

The sheriff replied, "I'm sorry, Mrs. McCormick, but the house was secured by a court order at the request of Mr. Lewis."

"It does not pertain to me. That is my house now and I would like the keys."

"I'm sorry; but I can't let you have them. You may talk to the judge, but I don't think it will do any good. The order was that the house was to be secured until after probate."

"He must have lost his damn mind. That is my house and you can't keep me out of it. If I have too, I'll break the damn lock."

"Please Mrs. McCormick, don't do that, it will only make matters worse."

"Just what in the hell would you do about it, arrest me?"

"I would if you forced me. If I did, I'm sure the judge would let you out to attend your Father's funeral." She and John stormed out of his office. They then went to the Herrington Hotel for a room to accommodate their stay in town.

The funeral service was Saturday afternoon. The sanctuary of First Baptist Church was filled almost to capacity. The front pew was reserved for family and the pall bearers. Railroad and his wife, Margie, were seated in the second pew.

After the first hymn, the family was escorted to their pew. Railroad rose from his seat and went to the podium. He removed a paper from his coat pocket and began to read. "Benjamin Thomas Lewis was born September 20, 1858 at The Lambertine Plantation in Magnolia Arkansas. He was preceded in death by his wife Marie DuPoint Lewis. He is survived by daughter, Sarah Marie McCormick and her husband Dr. John McCormick of Baltimore Md., one granddaughter Charlene Marie Bolton and her husband Robert John Bolton and one great grandson Benjamin John Bolton of Tulsa Oklahoma. He was preceded in death by his parents, John Thomas Lewis and Ann Cato Lewis, Sister Mary Ann Lewis and brother, Confederate Army Lieutenant Thomas P. Lewis."

Railroad folded the slip of paper, and having secured it within his breast pocket; he stepped back from the podium. Removing another scrap of paper from his pocket, he returned to the stand and began to deliver a eulogy. "Mr. Ben was the best friend I could possibly have. We sometimes called each other brother. When he was born, I was nine month old. His mother went to be with the Lord the next day after his birth. For the first few months of his life, he was nursed and cared for by a woman by the name of Castalee Dockery. She was my mother. During our childhood years, we ate at the same table, slept in the same bed and were schooled together until after the war. We were separated when he moved to Jefferson, Texas in 1866 at the age of eight. He graduated Jefferson High School in 1875 and attended Arkansas A & M College for one year before entering the Baltimore School of Business, in Baltimore, Md. There he met and married Marie DuPoint. He graduated in 1879 with a Law Degree and they moved to Amarillo in 1880. He and Marie were pillars of the community. The city of Amarillo has benefitted greatly by their presence. I know he will be missed by many people. For sure, I'll be one of them." He then stepped from the podium and returned to his seat.

When the service was over, the casket was opened and the guests, in single file, viewed the body and then greeted the family. Sarah turned and said, "Railroad come and sit with us, you're part of the family." Railroad began lightly crying and joined them on the first pew.

Railroad spotted Mr. Bronson and Marty in line waiting to view the body. He thought to himself, "This is interesting that Marty will shake hands with a sister and his mother and I'm the only living person who knows." He noticed that Sarah had focused her attention toward him. When he was shaking Charlene's hand, Railroad noticed the resemblance. They both had a full face, their noses were similar and the hair was blond with a light tent of red. He could also see that some features resembled Sarah. He thought to himself, "no one else will notice. The only reason I have is because I know the truth." Sarah looked at Marty with a puzzling expression on her face. She offered her right hand to him with the palm down. Marty placed his right hand under hers and then placed his left hand on top of hers. He said, "I am very sorry Mrs. McCormick, we will miss him." Sarah became speechless when she saw the two small fingers on his left hand. She stared at him as he was walking away, ignoring the next person in line for a moment. She regained her composer with thoughts of her mother's advice of thirty two years ago "Trust me. It's the best thing to do. He has a deformed left hand. No telling what other problems he may have."

After the visitor procession was over, Sarah rushed outside and scanned the crowd looking for Fred and Marty. They were nowhere in sight. She thought to herself, "That was my son. He looked about the correct age and he favored Charlene. What are the odds of two people near the same age having deformed fingers on their left hand? I'm sure Dad knew who he is. I hope I'm the only other person that knows his existence and no one must ever know."

After the burial, the crowd began to disburse and Sarah went to Railroad. "Railroad, who was that man with Mr. Bronson?"

"All I know is that he is one of Mr. Bronson's ranch hands. Fred can't see well enough to drive anymore and he drives him around."

"What is his name?"

Railroad, not wanting to give much information replied, "I can't remember his name, but I do remember he had an unusual last name."

"Oh well, I was just wondering. It's not important."

The next afternoon Sarah and John boarded the train for their journey back to Baltimore. John had planned to occupy his time on the long journey by reading. Sarah was emotionally exhausted. She sat next to John and cried very lightly. Her thoughts were of her recent encounter with her son, her father's death and the most disturbing incident concerning the locks on her father's home. There was no doubt that the lock out was Ben's way of getting even for the money problems they had caused him. After several hours of crying, she had begun to get on John's nerves. He looked at her and said in a stern voice, "My God, Sarah get over it. What we did, anyone else in their right mind would have done the same thing before he lost their money."

"She looked up at him and replied, "Railroad Dockery would have never done him that way."

****

June 20, 1936, all involved persons were notified to appear at Potter County Civil Court IV at two p. m. for the reading of the "Last Will and Testament of Benjamin John Lewis." The judge read the preliminary statements of the legal requirements of the filing. Ben, having a law degree, was meticulous and everything was in proper order.

The distributions of assets were as follows:

1. The City of Amarillo Parks Department, the sum of $1,000 for the development of "The Marie Lewis City Park".
2. Mary Smith, my friend and secretary, the sum of $1,000.
3. Ophelia Gomez, my friend and servant, the sum of $500.
4. Ruth Lightfoot, my friend and servant, the sum of $500.
5. Felix Garcia, my friend, caretaker and chauffer, the sum of $1,500 and my 1932 Ford Deluxe Roadster Automobile.
6. Railroad Dockery, my lifelong friend, the sum of $1,000 and my 1935 Fisher Town Car Sedan Automobile.
7. Sarah McCormick, my daughter and her husband, Dr. John McCormick of Baltimore Maryland, the sum of $100.

8. Charlene Bolton, my granddaughter of Tulsa Oklahoma, all my remaining assets, including but not limited to, my home and all furnishings located at 1101 Broadway Street, "The First Commerce Bank," "The Marie Lewis Cattle Company," all other commercial and residential real estate properties held by me.

Signed; Benjamin John Lewis

CHAPTER 27

Conclusion

Railroad Dockery died July 26, 1940 at eighty-six years and one month of age. His estate and the businesses "Railroad Dockery Salvage Company" and "Dockery Art Gallery" were left to his two sons and one daughter.

Fred William Bronson died August 10, 1941 at age eighty years of age. After he was laid to rest, Marty and Susan were very quiet on their trip back to the ranch. Finally Susan asked "What do we do now?"

"I have no idea. I guess we will be working for his niece and nephew soon."

"I didn't know about them. Were they at the funeral?"

"If they were, I wouldn't have known. I don't know them. I only heard him mention them a time or two. They live out of state. I'm sure that his executor will notify them of his death."

About two weeks later Marty received a registered letter stating that he was to appear in The Fifth Civil Court, Breckenridge,

Texas on August 24, 1941 at two o'clock p.m. for the reading of Fred William Bronson's "Last Will and Testimony." Jake Mangus and Bruce Rodgers, the ranch hands, also received a copy of the registered letter.

Marty, Susan, Jake and Bruce arrived in the court room a little early. A few moments later a court recorder entered. She introduced herself and sat at a desk near the Judge's bench. At almost two o'clock, three men entered and were seated at a table before the bench.

Susan whispered to Marty, "Do you know any of them?"

"I think one of them is Fred's banker. I don't know the others. They may be the niece and nephew's attorneys. I was expecting more people here."

The judge entered at precisely two o'clock. Everyone stood and he then asked that everyone be seated. He introduced the court recorder and then asks everyone to introduce themselves. The first man stood "I am Roland Smith, with the law firm of "Smith, Rodgers and Orr". I am executor of the last will and testament, acting on behalf of Fred William Bronson."

"My name is Grover Watson; I am president First National Bank of Breckenridge Texas."

The third man stood and said, "My name is Robert Mitchell. I am a clerk for Stephens County and my duties are to file these proceedings in all county records.

The judge then looked at Marty, Susan, Jake and Bruce. They stood and Marty said, "My name is Marty Clafcliff, and this is my wife Susan Calfcliff. We are here at the request of the court."

Jake stood and said, "My name is Jake Mangus, I am here at the request of the court."

Bruce stood and said, "My name is Bruce Rodgers and I'm also here as requested by the court."

"Thank you, please be seated. We are here for the reading of Fred William Bronson's last will and testament. Do any of you know of any person not present, that should be notified before the reading?"

Roland Smith stood and said, "All persons, requested by Mr. Bronson are present."

The judge preceded by stating his name, the court number, date and time for the benefit of the court recorder. He then unfolded the will and held it up for everyone to see. This is a hand written will, dated March 24, 1931, witnessed by three persons, notarized and recorded as required by Texas Law. He then began to read.

"Last Will and Testament of Fred William Bronson"

"I, Fred William Bronson, in the county of Stephens in the state of Texas, knowing it is allowed for all men to die and being of sound and disposing mind and memory, do make and publish this as my last will and testament, revoking all others heretofore made by me.

At my death, I desire to be buried near my family where a plot is available at Oak Hill Cemetery in a manor becoming my position and means.

I desire all my just debts to be paid in as short a time as can be done with justice to my benefactor.

I give and bequest to my ranch hand Bruce Rodgers the sum of $1000.

I give and bequest to my ranch hand Jake Mangus the sum of $1000.

I give and bequest to my ranch foreman Marty Clafcliff the remainder of my estate, all ranch properties and personal properties, including any other assets acquired after the date of this document.

Signed "Fred William Bronson" Dated March 24, 1931.

The judge said, "This document contains the required and notarized signatures of two witnesses as required by the state of

Texas. This document was recorded by Dave Dixon, County Clerk, Stephens County Texas and his authorizing seal was attached and dated March 24, 1931. I have thoroughly reviewed this document and rule by the power invested to me as Probate Judge of Stephens County Texas that all legal requirements have been fulfilled." He then added, "All assets of the estate of Fred William Bronson are frozen for a minimum of thirty days and not to exceed ninety days. A temporary account has been set up with Mr. Grover Watson of the First National Bank of Breckenridge, Texas and all funding of ranch operations will be distributed by Roland Smith, executor of the estate. All other assets, being ranch or personal, must remain on the premises until the date of distribution."

The judge then stood and said, "The Fifth Civil Probate Court of Texas is now adjourned." He hit the gavel, turned and walked away.

Marty and Susan sat very quietly, not believing what they had just heard. Marty looked at Susan as tears began to run down her face. "Why are you crying, you should be smiling?"

"This is a dream come true and I don't know why."

"I can't believe it myself. Let's get out of here." As they stood to leave, they were met by Mr. Roland Smith.

"I have been Fred's attorney for a number of years. I will be happy to continue to handle your affairs, although you may want your personal attorney. I will understand. We have a ton of papers to sign, notarize and file with the county and state. We can't file for thirty days but it will be nice to have all this taken care of when the time comes. I will be free next Wednesday afternoon. Could you come by my office?" He then handed Marty a business card.

"Let's get the show on the road. I'll see you Wednesday," Marty said with a grin as he and Susan walked away. When they got into the truck, they sat for a while without saying anything.

Finally Susan said, "Are we going to sit here all afternoon or we going to our ranch?"

"We're not going to our ranch yet, we are going to the cemetery, and I got to talk to Fred."

Susan said with a smile, "He won't talk to you. If you start asking questions, he may send you back to Hondo."

"I don't have that threat hanging over me anymore, although he told me many times he knew people in high places."

They parked at the cemetery and Marty got out of the truck. Susan asked, "Do you want me to come with you or would you rather be alone."

"Don't be silly, come with me. He has pissed me off and I'm going to give him a piece of my mind."

They walked to the grave site and Marty sat on the headstone which was placed there shortly after Fred's wife had died. He looked at the freshly turned clay dirt and said, "Fred thanks for being so generous. I don't know why you always had to be so damn secretive. You said you knew people in high places, I guess you really do. What really upsets me today is the fact that you had written your will fifteen days before I was released. You had never seen me, as far as I know. There is only one reason you would have chosen me. I have known all my life that I was adopted. I have never thought about my biological parents. As far as I'm concerned, my dad is a cripple who fell from a windmill and my mother is a woman who cried herself to sleep every night that I was incarcerated. Fred, I know your generosity has something to do with my biological parents. Your son, Joe was killed three years before I was born. I know he had nothing to do with it. Denton was too young to be my father when he died and you are just too damn ugly. Well Fred, I will accept things as they are and ask no more questions. Thanks Fred." He stood, reached for Susan's hand and said, "Let's go enjoy our Broken Spur Ranch. What do ye think about us making some babies? We will need ranch hands some day."

She smiled and said, "Let's go home."

The "Broken Spur Ranch" is now owned and operated by Fred Calfcliff and Bronson Calfcliff, the sons of the late Marty and Susan Clafcliff.